BEECHAM'S INFIRMARY FOR THE AFFLUENT AFFLICTED

MY DARLING MALADY #1

BEECHAM'S INFIRMARY FOR THE AFFLUENT AFFLICTED

A Gothic Paranormal Romance Novella by

BRIAR SOMERSET

Cover Design by: @Soren.Designs

Interior Formatting: Briar Somerset

Character Art: @Elleillustrationss

Digital ISBN-13: 979-8-9873284-8-4

Print ISBN-13: 979-8264292873

Sonder & Serum Special Edition Print ISBN: 9798269410364

Audio ISBN-13:

IN THIS BOOK, YOU'LL FIND...

Content Warning:
Death of a minor (off page)
Pandemic/ epidemic themes
Body horror
Medical suspense and dental mutilation
Conversations surrounding grief and loss
Open door romance
Blood Kink

Tropes & Microtropes:
Autumnal Victorian London Setting
Diverse Romance
Gothic Mystery
30+ year-old MCs
Virgin FMC
Caregiver Rep
Mutual Comfort/ Corruption
Vampires & Supernatural Creatures

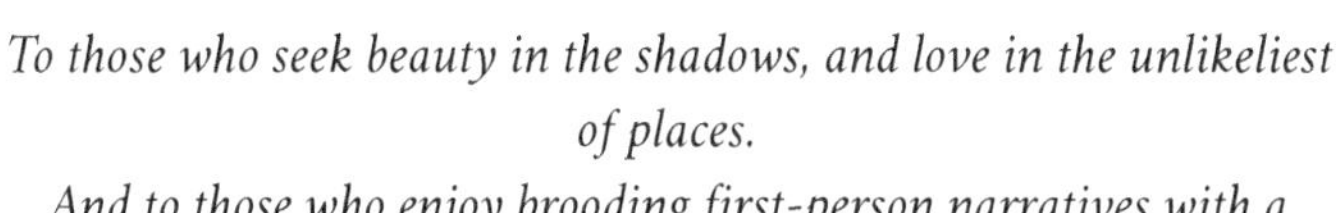

To those who seek beauty in the shadows, and love in the unlikeliest of places.
And to those who enjoy brooding first-person narratives with a dash of French introspection, I suppose.

Man is not truly one, but truly two.

— ROBERT LOUIS STEVENSON, *THE STRANGE
CASE OF DR. JEKYLL AND MR. HYDE*

Beecham's Infirmary for the Affluent Afflicted started as a 7,400 word short story that blossomed into a tale riddled with longing and disease. Monsieur Valmont and Miss Castro-Tan have occupied my thoughts for some time now, and it is a pleasure (and relief) to finally offer their story to you.

The novella you hold in your hands contains a narrative hastily written in the frigid months before the world shut down, shaped by suspicion and Victorian unease—where devotion blooms like a patch of blood upon one's cream blouse, and not all ailments are mortal.

This is the first installment in the *My Darling Malady* series, a collection of gothic novellas following Jacques and Annie as they navigate the peculiar tragedies of our world. An immersive audiobook will be released in late 2025, designed to complement the story with voice and atmosphere.

May you find something here of succor and sin that lingers long after the page, much like jasmine on the throat. Or blood on the tongue.

CHAPTER 1

IN WHICH A STRANGER ARRIVES, TEETH
ARE DELIVERED BY POST, AND POLITENESS
PROVES USELESS

*W*estminster, 1849

"So," the constable shouts over his shoulder. "Paris, I hear."

These are the first words he utters since we'd left Scotland Yard, where the looks I'd received were nothing short of welcoming.

Wonderful! The newcomer. Give him the Piccadilly couple!

Upon my summoning, I'd hoped for something challenging. A case to test the limits of body and mind and bring one of society's many monsters to some sort of justice. A difference-maker of a job. Instead, I'd been handed an assignment meant only to quell the trivial concerns of the bourgeoisie.

I give a nod that he can't see through the bustling crowd. Paris, yes. Saint-Germain specifically, but my past is none of his business—nor anyone's, if I've anything to say about it. This is a new beginning, and it belongs to no one but me, born anew the moment I had arrived in London the prior evening.

"You're young for a private investigator." It isn't quite a

question, but he fires off more of them before I can answer. An attempt to unsettle me. "Thirties? Any family in the area?"

"A great-great uncle in Penzance, though he moved here from Cornouaille, or so I've heard. And no, none of my own —no partner, nor children." I think that's what he's asking. What a strange way to phrase his question. "I'll be thirty-three this autumn."

"Soon, then."

It's actually thirty-three *next* autumn, but that does little to offset my lack of tenure, or the stubborn ghost of a beard that never quite commits to growing in. "I apprenticed for a couple years before opening my own inquiry office last May."

"Your mentorship must've been an impressive one, then." It's not a compliment. Not the way he means it. He shoots an incredulous glance back at me, as if he must be missing something. He's probably wondering why his commissioner handpicked me.

Not to fret; over the two-day trip here, it's all I've pondered.

"My father was one of the best." A man for the people. Not a former cop nor serviceman. He painted and travelled before returning home at his parents' wishes, determined to break into a trade. So, he did, and made it his life's work. The case we'd last collaborated on was the last time I saw him alive. I leave this part out, and the constable doesn't bother to ask.

He pushes forward, already disinterested.

A low brontide rolls across the canopy of clouds. I barely keep up with his bobbing helmet amidst the throng of top hats and bonnets as we scurry across Butcher Row. Someone coughs beside me—a wet sound that has me pressing my folded handkerchief against my face. I don't need to turn to know the woman beside me just rasped a handful of blood into her napkin.

You're sick. Stay inside. It's what the doctors back home would say.

D'après le journal quotidien, les Parlementaires demeurent un chef de file mondial en matière de science et de médecine en progrès. Apparemment.

"Has London treated you fairly?" shouts the constable.

"So far." I've not been in town for a day, yet the chemical plumes from the textile mills and the lingering aroma of horse shit have already made a distinct impression in the form of a pounding headache in my forehead and jaw. From what I know of the place, this is among its fairer treatment of new arrivals. Clutching my hat, I put my head down, avoiding several other hacking residents as I pardon myself through the crowded street to catch up to him.

It's my turn to ask questions. The constable hasn't prodded too much, but if I monopolize the conversation, the less opportunity he has to pick at the details of my life. Paris is all he needs to know.

"Is this the right way to the Piccadilly couple?" I recall the map at the station. We're headed east. "Isn't it behind us?"

"Yes, but—*right, excuse us,*" he grumbles, before taking a sharp turn onto Gill Street, which, in comparison to the streets around The Yard, is a cobblestone-veined thoroughfare of high traffic indeed. I pivot to follow him and barely dodge a carriage and tittering crowd of soot-dusted children on their lunch hour. "We aren't headed to their home. I'm bringing you to the crime scene." Noticing my brows rise, he grins through his mustache. "You did say you were eager to start."

"I assumed it was theft." It was usually a matter of robbery with the sort of couple residing in an area like Piccadilly. I'd assumed such, considering the urgent manner in which my presence had been requested. Shaken awake by my own authorities and on a train to Calais not an hour later. "Stolen pearls. A ransacked cupboard."

"No pearls amiss this time." The constable comes to a halt so abruptly that I bump into him; he doesn't seem to notice, or if he does, he doesn't care. We've arrived at an unmarked door, the first on a row of brownstone establishments. To its left sits a shop boasting a variety of fine hats and silk scarves in the long window, its name spelt across the front in ostentatious lettering.

Lewis & Allenby.

"What was stolen, then?"

The constable turns to me, but is interrupted by a woman's frantic cry.

"Oh, Charles. I can't bear it!"

A couple emerges from the street and makes a beeline for us. The gentleman offers an outstretched hand to the constable while his grief-stricken beloved hangs for dear life onto his opposite arm. She shoots me a filthy look.

I divert my gaze and stuff my hands into my trouser pockets, already uncomfortable. What did they lose? An entire fortune?

"I can't bear to look," the woman chokes at the door before us, then smears her face in her Charles's lapel.

"Sergeant Lewis," Charles says curtly. Sergeant, *then.* A trained, warm tone, despite everything. The slack in his posture and lack of a morning coat tells me he's not quite a Parliament man. A magistrate, maybe? No, no case tucked under his arm, either.

Sergeant Lewis returns Charles's handshake with a tight squeeze. "Charles, Blanche. Good day. This is—" Lewis frowns and tilts his head back at me, now offering me *his* hand.

I'd rather wade through a charnel house than shake hands with a constable—or sergeant, or whatever.

Pretending not to notice, I already know what he's going to ask; yes, he *did* get my name back at the office. No, I don't care that he doesn't remember it, because I hadn't cared enough to ask for his.

"Jacques, sir." I give Charles and Blanche a smile I hope passes as warmth. Despite the rays of sun peeking through a lapse in the clouds, a chill passes through me.

Charles doesn't respond, looking most displeased as he fixes the end of his mustache. "Sergeant. A moment, if you will?"

Lewis nods and cocks his head at me, and I gladly excuse myself to the stoop. They don't bother speaking softly—I can hear every word.

"I apologize for stepping out of line, but this is preposterous. First, your commissioner refuses to help. And then, when he finally agrees to accommodate us, you bring me an amateur."

My vision clouds crimson.

My father was Étienne Valmont—my grandfather, Gaspard, Comte de Valmont, you insipid swine, I want to snap. The urge claws up my throat, unbidden. But I swallow it. No one knows our surname here; the one that once opened hospital doors and carried enough weight to fund entire wards in France now means less than the stone beneath my shoes.

A noble family of sturdy name and medical patronage. A family crest, even, in the shape of a serpent-twined blade—a clever play off of the Rod of Asclepius, by some ancestor with an apparent sense of humor. My father renounced it all before I was born. Then, Gaspard died of a winter illness, and what little weight our surname held faded into obscurity.

And here I stand, heir to a disgraced title, having wasted my brief tenure at the Faculté de Droit on absinthe and cards and women, to my grandmother's silent disappointment.

Picked up my father's trade on a whim rather than a calling, and ended up shipped overseas like some sniffing dog, all to be spat upon by London's authorities and elites alike.

I lift my gaze to the shop window, feigning interest in the cut of a coat or the shimmer of silk. Anything to avoid the itch in my palms. I trace the grooves in the brick with my eyes, counting them to breathe through the urge to splatter Charles's innards across them.

"Charles," Lewis whispers pleadingly. "As we discussed yesterday, our hands are tied with other matters at the moment. Larger robberies. Two jewelers in Hatton Garden late last week. Handfuls of diamonds, gone." He snaps his fingers. "Just like that. There was another heist up the street last night. And the alleyway murders, which you might've read about."

"You think I care about diamonds? My father owns half of Portsman Square!"

Ah, oui. Car rien n'exprime l'urgence morale comme l'héritage d'une propriété à Marylebone.

"What about the outsourcing you mentioned?" Charles throws his hands out to his sides, gesturing towards any option but me. "You must help us find our daughter."

There it is. The one thing more prized than a fortune.

"That's the thing," Lewis replies, raising his voice for me to hear. "We *have* outsourced. Jacques has traveled here all the way from Paris." He turns to look at me. "Isn't that right?"

Indeed, I've spent the past thirty-six hours on trains, a ferry, and more trains. After three hours of sleep, rushed to Scotland Yard on a hackney. "I have," I confirm, as if my accent hasn't given it away. "Rest assured, we will find your daughter."

Blanche pales even further. Charles glares at Lewis, furious tears forming at the corners of his own eyes.

"Unfortunately," Lewis is quick to add, "I haven't yet had a chance to inform Monsieur Valmont of the finer details. He arrived at the office early this morning and was so eager to start."

"Perfect. A foreigner who doesn't even know *what* he's investigating."

"If I may," I interject. Lewis is *not* about to pin this on me. "I apologize if there's been a misunderstanding. You see, I'm the private investigator in charge of your case from this point on. Any details may be shared with me in confidence."

At this, Charles's mustache stops quivering, and he's a little less red. "A *private* investigator?"

"Yes. Now, keep in mind, I don't make any arrests or prosecutions." I stride slowly to them, so as not to spook his glaring wife. "Instead, I am tasked with acquiring crucial information as quickly as possible, by any means necessary. With my findings and your cooperation, a decision is made on how to proceed. Sergeant Lewis here was only showing me the way, since I am new to your town." Lewis has only complicated these matters, as far as I'm concerned. I give the couple a consoling smile and eye the busy streets, which start to clear with the workday resuming. "He was about to be on his way. Isn't that right?"

The three of them eye me in suspicion, as if Lewis didn't expect someone who knew how to do their job when his commissioner contacted my office.

"Precisely," Lewis finally agrees. Despite his skepticism, the relief is plain on his face. "Monsieur Valmont. Mr and Mrs Wharncliffe. Good day, and best of luck."

With a nod toward me and the couple, he tips his hat and disappears down the steps and into the crowd like a mongrel with its tail between his legs.

"Back to your daughter," I say, refocusing the discussion on what has become a belatedly urgent matter. "In a missing person's case, we have a narrow window of time if we are to find her—"

"We will be doing no such thing, because she is dead as nails." Charles's murky eyes bore into mine and I fight the urge to look down.

"I see." This changes things entirely. If I'd had time to find my cap in my luggage this morning, I would've removed it. How horrible. "Elaborate, if you will."

"Six days ago, our Alma showed the early signs of Consumption. Cold, even sitting at the hearth. Nose and cheeks scarlet. She let out a cough five days ago that was tinged red. We've both seen enough of this plague to know it doesn't take long for things to turn for the worst. So, by early next morning, we'd brought her here. That was the last time we saw her."

Four days ago, they'd seen her. "Pardon. Here?"

"Yes." Charles motions toward the doorframe his wife has slumped against like a stray cat begging to be let in. "Beecham's Infirmary."

I step back, and, for the first time since we arrived, take a good look at the doorstep. Unlike the other shops, it's nondescript, and looks nothing like a sanatorium. The two levels stacked above the peeling door are thin, barely enough room for anything more than an office, much less a chemist.

"Infirmary?" I'm dubious, unable to conceal my taut grimace. "In there?"

"It's exclusive, you buffoon!" Blanche glares up at me. "This infirmary offers cures most cannot afford." She pauses to hiccup between sobs, blowing her nose on her sleeve. "And we can most *certainly* afford them. Our Alma didn't deserve this. It just isn't fair."

"I hate to ask you to relive this, I know it must be painful. But could you please tell me," I say gently, "if you haven't seen her, what events have transpired to make you believe she's dead?"

Charles reaches into his coat pocket and retrieves a crumpled piece of paper, holding it out to me in his gloved hand.

I accept it without question and unfurl a faded photo of a cherub-faced girl of about ten, along with four small objects that roll over my palm like dice. Two of them glint in the sunlight.

They aren't dice at all.

"Where did you—" I stagger for the banister, my lip curling as I press the bundle back into Charles's expectant palm.

He fishes around and holds a single tooth up, the roots still stained red. "The courier delivered this that same evening."

"You're sure they're hers?"

"Yes. Those are her amalgam fillings."

Charles then pockets his grim findings and brandishes a piece of folded parchment at me, which I accept as a welcome distraction.

Mr. and Mrs. Wharncliffe,

We sincerely regret to inform you of your dearest Alma's passing. Her demise was unforeseen, as her condition worsened rapidly the day of her death. Here are her available remains, the rest of which have been donated to the noble cause of scientific research.

Our condolences and prayers are with you.

Your humble servant,

A. BEECHAM

I can barely reread the letter before Charles snatches it back, cradling it to his chest as if it is the last tangible memory of her, save the teeth. I take a moment to recompose myself as they both stare expectantly at me.

Detective work is a curious venture. It requires striking the perfect balance between indifference and concern. Compassion and clinical poise. In this instance, my unadulterated empathy pushes me to dig deeper. "And you don't believe this is what happened to her?"

They exchange glances.

"We don't know what to believe," replies Blanche.

"You showed *this* to the police, and they didn't believe you?"

"They grew unconcerned after reading the letter."

Bastards. They didn't have a missing girl to find alive. "Have you engaged with the infirmary since?"

Another roll of thunder grinds through the darkening clouds. "We've tried," says Charles. "Apparently, they don't let anyone who's not of poor health past the intake."

"What time was it delivered? Your letter, the day she was pronounced dead."

"A little past six," Blanche answers brusquely.

"And which one of you received it?"

"I did, but we didn't know of its contents until Charles opened it."

"Do you usually retrieve the evening mail, Mrs Wharncliffe?" It is customary, especially in the evenings, for the husband to answer the door. Couriers, after all, come and go at all hours—though I'm under the impression the residents of Piccadilly are afforded prime mail hours, if not the earliest.

"Not usually," Blanche replies, face flushing. "But Charles was out."

"Does he normally stay out past…" I trail off, glancing between them both.

The shadows beneath their eyes are suddenly more noticeable. Charles steps forward to place himself between me and his wife, and Blanche is now completely removed from our exchange. Trembling, she cups her hand against the breeze to light the pipe she's procured from God knows where.

I run my hand over my face. They aren't suspects. Just a pair of exhausted parents in dire need of sleep and some answers. Two individuals thrust into the sudden misfortune of loss, just as I've been.

"My humblest apologies." As if on cue, a raindrop grazes my knuckle. "I've forgotten my place."

"You *dare* question us. You should be in there!" Charles jabs a finger toward the infirmary door before his hands go to his hair. He turns to Blanche, no longer addressing me. "After all of the funds my parents poured into this city, this is what we get in return. A juvenile detective."

Frustration surges through me at his words, at my overestimating my own ability and thinking I could do this a month after my father's demise.

Not when I'd received no answers myself. Not when I'd escaped by the hair of my teeth.

Charles is an angry father, he has every right to be, but barging outright into Beecham's Infirmary would prove useless. Just what was I supposed to ask?

Show me the Wharncliffe girl's corpse! And why the fuck are her teeth missing?

I could try, but it was likely they'd require the kind of warrant that only the department could give me, and not without pushback. This investigation required stealth—not the usual bedlam of the Yard's constables.

The tinny ring of a bell breaks the silence; behind

Charles, a carriage has parked. A tissue-clutching older woman and her coach driver have made their way into the shop next door.

Right, then. We'll start with the neighbor.

"Monsieur Wharncliffe." I tip my proverbial hat and begin retreating. "Madame Wharncliffe. I'll be commencing my investigation immediately."

"Where do you think you're going?" Charles snarls as I step back onto the sidewalk, barely dodging a man and his bumbling beagle. "The infirmary is in there!"

I wave my hands and cup my ears, pretend I can't hear him, then shrug. What can I say? English is not my first language. "I'll be in touch within twenty-four hours, you can be sure of it. Expect to hear from myself or Lewis!"

CHAPTER 2

IN WHICH HEATSTROKE IS MISTAKEN FOR FLIRTATION, FLIRTATION FOR ESPIONAGE, AND I AM THREATENED WITH TAILORING SHEARS

The bell sounds a second time as the door latches shut behind me, and I'm greeted with an overwhelming sense of midday London aristocracy. It takes a moment for my vision to fully adjust from pale sunlight to the dim interior, but there are shapes. Mirrors and mannequins at the back. Rows of silks and fabrics.

A perfect afternoon for the dawdling upper class.

Except, when it does—not one, nor two, but *eight* bonneted heads snap in my direction. The woman who'd entered before me glances up and sighs, muttering something about police work.

"Just a moment," a disembodied voice calls from the room beyond the register to my right, and I crane my head, trying to place its flustered source.

I'm about to go to the counter, but an elderly man seemingly materializes out of nowhere, obscuring my view.

"Sir," he mutters, tipping his tall hat and peering at me through his thick spectacles. "I understand you have a job to do, but the ladies wish to shop in peace. Also, there is a rule about the police working off-duty." He glances me up and down. "Or lacking uniform."

"While I wholeheartedly agree, I am not the police." I watch his eyes widen—then narrow—at my accent. "I'm an investigator. There's been a disappearance next door. Are you the owner?"

"No, I'm one of the tailors. Our shop owners are out today, but—"

"You can leave him, Thomas. I'll handle it." The disembodied voice returns, and Thomas utters an apology before sauntering over to the customers, ushering their attention back to the mirrors.

As soon as he's out of view, a pair of hands plop a towering, teetering stack of dyed silks ranging from cream to a deep crimson onto the counter. The person those hands belong to sprouts up from behind it like a weed.

"I'm in charge today," she announces, with squared shoulders and the steeled smile of a shop owner—one assessing enough to make my heart skip—despite the several pins protruding from her smock sleeve and patch of soot upon her freckle-dusted nose.

"You're not Lewis," I observe. "Nor Allenby."

"And you're not English."

Her tone is just short of cordial, but her large brown eyes study me unabashedly. Her dark hair is pulled back into a sleek bun, held with a silk ribbon, save for the pieces that brush her cheeks.

Maintaining a straight face is almost as difficult as refraining from replying, *Neither are you.*

"And how may I help you?" Her voice tightens.

I don't realize I'm staring. I hastily dip into a bow. "My apologies. I was just passing through."

The seamstress responds with a polite clear of the throat

that is an evident ruse, because she beckons me threateningly forward with one finger. Her skin, rich with the complexion of aged amber, is flushed deliciously pink. I'd be a fool not to oblige; without question, I step to the counter. In all the fuss of the afternoon, I'd almost forgotten my headache, but the pain rails relentlessly into my skull as I close the space between us.

The woman takes it a step further, leaning forward so that our faces are a breath apart, and I think for one ludicrous second she might kiss me. She smells immediately of jasmine and anise. I'm about to comment on it when her hand darts out. She grips me by the lapel and tugs me to her, causing me to lose balance and my palms to slap the counter.

"You wanted to snoop," she growls. "I don't need you announcing the nature of your investigation to all of my customers. If this affects business, they won't find what's left of you in the Thames. You're frightening the entire shop."

My ears have grown atrociously hot; I can sense a multitude of eyes on us. "You're the one frightening *me*."

"Why? Is it because I am the head of the shop, and not the soft-spoken one in the tall hat?"

"That depends. Is accosting strangers a favorite pastime of yours?" I raise my hand slowly, gently toward hers, but she catches it and presses her fingers into the tendons at my wrist, rendering it slack before forcing it back onto the table. She shouldn't know how to disarm me, yet something in the precision of her movement tells me she's trained to deal with men. "What about attacking investigators?"

"Only the ones who come sniffing where they shouldn't."

"What is your name?" I ask, determined not to break her glare.

"What are you going to do, arrest me?"

I won't—I can't make arrests—but my eyes linger upon

her wrists. There's a jade bracelet on one of them, adorned with a golden clasp. "I at least deserve to know the name of the woman throttling me."

In truth, I don't blame her for reacting this way. I'm a stranger. An unwelcome entity in her shop. Perhaps someone once made her feel the same, or the ones who came before her.

The gaslamp above us flares as if it can sense the tension between us. I should pull away. I should say something clever. But all I can think of is how close her mouth is to mine, the heady aroma wafting off of her skin in the brick-trapped heat, and how odd it is that fear and fascination rouse twin beasts within me.

Perhaps she senses it, too, because she roughly releases me and steps back across the counter, studying me distrustfully. "What is it that you want?"

"There's been a disappearance at the infirmary next door. A young girl was reported dead four days ago, but her parents are suspicious, as they've not been permitted to see her."

I glimpse something like recognition—but only for a moment. "And what do you want me to do about that? People die all the time at infirmaries. In their own beds. You cough one day and are gone the next."

Now, I'm the one leaning in to whisper. "Have you noticed anything strange about the infirmary?"

"You're not from here." She takes my silence as confirmation. "Everything about it is strange. Beecham's Infirmary is fairly new."

A glance out the window tells me the streets are emptying. There are more carriages now than pedestrians. I spot the corner of the crumbling steps. If they haven't been here long, no attempt at restoration has been made. "How new?"

"A few weeks. A month, if that. Rumor has it, all the other hospitals—Royal, King's, Bartholomew's—are filled to the brim with the dead and dying. There's no space left."

Things were bad back home, but I don't recall it being this dire. "Do people not recover?"

"These days, our hospitals aren't places of healing so much as they are gateways to the end. For every person who's made the journey to recovery, they infect two to three people along the way. Beecham came in with a promise to change that, catering to those requiring mild treatment or convalescent care. Those who can pay for it, that is."

I scoff, disgusted. "Already swindling the public and they've been here a month? That's quick."

"There was nothing for them to build. The space was vacant, an old shop. All they had to do was knock some walls down. The pounding went on for days." She peeks over my shoulder at her preoccupied customers. "They want Lewis & Allenby's as well, but my bosses are holding firm."

"What does he look like? This Beecham?"

"That's the thing," she says, leaning in to whisper. I'm glad she's cooperating, albeit begrudgingly. "No one's seen him, so far as I know. No one in our shop, anyway. He's some sort of entrepreneur surgeon, with very little time to spare. He contacted us one time by letter, and that's it."

That was the ticket. It was commonplace for business owners to reside in their offices during the work week. Some of them lived there. But, disappearing bodies—supposed donation? Lack of presence? There was surely something sinister occurring within the brick walls behind her, and that's what the Wharncliffe case would reveal.

While I couldn't promise the recovery of poor Alma's remains, especially if they'd already been sold or donated to researchers, I could at least shed light on their ill practices and hopefully prevent it from happening to anyone else.

"In your time here, have you ever seen folks enter? Visitors?"

Her brows furrow. "Families drop off their infected, I suppose."

"Have you ever seen the ill leave? After their stay?"

The seamstress scowls, as if she's realized she's being questioned, scooping an armful of the fabric and turning her back to me to place them on the far counter. "People aren't strolling in and out, if that's what you're asking. Casual visitors are prohibited. It *is* a sanatorium, after all."

This made sense. London, as it seemed, received the brunt of most ailments these days. Still, harvesting corpses without consent was illegal.

"I need to get in."

She snorts. "Good luck, detective."

"Private *investigator*," I correct, with no intention of leaving. "Jacques. And I could use your help, Seamstress."

She doesn't give her name in return. She's busied herself separating the silk by color, but the tips of her ears peeking out from her hair are pink. "I won't get involved."

I shove my hand in my pocket. "You know, as a plainclothes detective, I could use a new pair of trousers or two. Since you and your fellow tailor are running the shop today, I presume the owners are out?"

"Away on business, yes. And Thomas is doing no such thing. I'm in charge when they're away." She slips a pair of large tailoring shears from her skirt pocket and begins to cut through a piece of fabric. "My career is set here. And you'll have to make an appointment for me to fit you into new trousers."

"Which is exactly why you should help me infiltrate. Yet another perfect opportunity for us to see each other again."

She is evidently not bemused by my charms, not bothering

a glance in my direction. "If Beecham discovers I or anyone else from the shop is involved, he'll buy us outright. He already offered a ridiculous amount of money. Our owners might've declined, but that's because they were in longstanding business with the royal family. All he has to do is pull a few strings. Offer funds to the right people, and we're done for. Evicted. With this space, he'd open an entire operating hospital, fronting nurse and surgeon wages within a week," she replies frostily as I nod, retreating from the counter. I bend my head to hide my grin. "Everything we've worked for, gone. Everything my mother sacrificed her safety for, gone. And, by the way, breaking into a sanatorium sounds illegal."

I round her counter just as she whirls to face me. "So is selling corpses for research. Or giving them away without written consent of the family."

Her fingers tense around the shears. There's a minuscule tremble at her wrist. "How do *you* know that's what's happening?"

"The letter disclosing the girl's demise informed her parents that her body was donated. Enclosed in the parcel were four of her teeth." I let that settle. "That's all they have to remember her by."

Her cruel laugh is the biting sound of disbelief. "That sounds like an unfortunate case of failing to scour the fine print."

"That is not something one discloses in fine print," I snap. "Especially when families trust you with their dying." Her mouth tightens. "If I get in, I might be able to shut it down. Which means Lewis & Allenby stays. Beecham loses. And you—" I let my gaze flick across the room, the rolls of silk, fine dresses and hats in tidy order. "You keep your mother's legacy."

She's already stepping closer, the shears swinging lightly

in her grasp. "This is not her legacy. What I make of myself on a shore she never chose to land on, is."

I fall silent, biting my tongue. The trade routes. Merchant ships. A young woman, taken or traded. Tea, silk, opium. Bodies. Any of them are plausible, and it's not my place to ask, but my jaw tightens.

"And if you don't get in?" she presses.

My gaze falls to the shears, which she's lifted to her hip like a knife. "If not…" I take a breath, and I'm aware of my voice softening. "Then I suppose I'd have no choice but to report your refusal to cooperate. Which would be… unfortunate."

The seamstress freezes.

"The Yard would investigate. Top to bottom, every ledger, every receipt. Every little secret you, Lewis and Allenby, your mother, and your fellow tailors might have stitched into these very walls."

I'm not serious, of course. I abhor the police and everything they stand for—hate that my father worked somewhat alongside them when he had to. They serve whomever wears the heavier boot with no real or refined sense of honor.

I realize the error in my empty threat as her eyes burn with hatred. Unblinking, as if she wants to set me on fire. She lifts the shears. Not threateningly, not yet. But high enough, and my lips uncontrollably twitch.

I'm abhorrent, I'm entirely aware. A reluctant investigator —I never said I was a good person. One might even argue my profession is proof of my moral ambiguity. But the way she wields her tool-turned-weapon and the thought of her brandishing it at me does something most foul to my raging senses.

A sudden burst behind my temples, like something inside me is cracking open.

I blink. Once. Twice, and violet spots dance before me. The room is tilting. My lips curl before I can stop them.

It's wrong, this is all wrong.

But there's something in the way the seamstress holds the shears—her sheer defiance and scorching fury—that sets something rotten and wired humming beneath my skin. My stomach lurches, and in time with my pounding head, my ears begin to ring.

I want to touch her. To run.

Heat floods my chest, then my neck, like steam building with nowhere to go. Suddenly, the shop is sweltering. The fabrics and silks glimmer behind her like water. The seamstress is shouting, but I can't make out what she's saying. A high whine has filled my ears, and the sound of my father's wails drowns everything out.

I reach out for her, not for balance, but on instinct. Something—someone—to anchor myself to.

Before I know it, she's cussing at me, the shears are shoved into her pocket, and my hands are in hers.

"Is this your way of getting me to comply? Falling into my arms?" she pants, tugging me out into the street.

My arm tucked in hers, she tugs me out into the early evening. The air isn't as stifling here, the heat lessened by the breeze. I gulp it down, unable to answer, not entirely sure what she's asking. All I know is that she looks disarmingly beautiful in the checkered flat cap she's pulled on after removing the ribbon from her hair, which cascades in loose curls and waves around her collarbone like a fragrant scarf. The wool of the tawny coat she donned is scratchy but warm against my thin shirt.

"Well?" Her eyes dart to the road, yanking me across it. I

would check for carriages and horses, too, if a wave of violent nausea hadn't momentarily consumed me. "Were you going to have me arrested for refusing to talk to you?"

She needs to know that she can trust me.

"No," I manage honestly as she pulls me along. "I was never going to do that. I was going to propose I act as your boss's lawyer, or a magistrate—to go into the infirmary expressing interest in their offer. It's the only way they'd let me in."

"That isn't the only way, but it *is* how we'd get pinned for fraud. I'm not meddling in legal affairs that aren't mine. This is how someone like me gets jailed, or worse," she snaps, suddenly looking ready to throw me in front of a passing carriage. "If you want a scapegoat, you are talking to the wrong person."

I fall silent and fix my bewildered expression, following her until we stop at a corner.

She stares at me long and hard. "Tell me, Jacques. What business do I have helping a town that wants nothing of people like me, except for wherever it suits them? When we're sewing their clothes, cleaning their streets. Do you really think I owe London a thing? It can choke."

Despite her evident resentment, there's a glimmer in her eyes. As if she expects an answer.

I bow my head in understanding. "For all their airs of civility, the English easily rival the Americans in their appetite for targeted scandal and their disdain for the foreigner. Fortunately for you, I am French."

She makes a sound of disgust and untangles our arms, and I resist the urge to reach for her again. "The malpractice at Beecham's goes far beyond their ability or inability to heal its residents Miss—"

"Annie Castro-Tan."

"*Annie*," I repeat. "Consumption is a terrible illness as it is.

The town is drowning in blood. Your useless police are preoccupied with God knows what, and people are disappearing."

"They are not *my* police," she says scathingly. "And those people are dying. Maybe it's their god punishing them for all of the pillaging and conquering they've done. You have no proof of anything else."

"I'm not sure what is happening behind those doors," I continue over her, growing impassioned, "but I'm certain of one thing—the sick cannot fend for themselves." Annie's expression is unreadable. "Neither can children. There is a family who lost their daughter and was robbed of closure. I was called from across the Channel to tend to them. My own father, a detective himself, was murdered last month when we were on the job. Impaled—it was barbaric," I hear myself admitting, and I wonder why I feel the need to open up to this complete stranger, to tear open these wounds so willingly. "The pain of losing someone important to you without answers is like nothing else. It haunts a person for a lifetime. If I am able to help, I will. I'll do it alone if I must."

An uncomfortable silence hangs between us, and several passersby stop their hacking to regard us curiously.

Annie's eyes search mine from above her scarf of hair, and I can sense her deliberating.

"And you'll do anything?" she asks.

"Anything."

She sighs, aggravated, and breaks into a brisk walk in the opposite direction of the flowing crowd.

"Follow me," she calls. "It's not far. And have you brought a handkerchief?"

Easily following her hat and matching her stride, I'm already reaching into my shirt pocket for it. Necessary for entering the larger crowds. "Of course. The air here is atrocious." I frown. "What's not far?"

Annie reaches over to snatch the cloth square out of my hand. I scramble for it, but the tissue is already gone, twirling away into the wind.

"What is *wrong* with you?"

She beckons me into the coughing crowds filing out of the mills. "How else do you think you're getting into Beecham's?"

CHAPTER 3

IN WHICH RICE PORRIDGE IS HAD—THUS, I FORGET MYSELF, MY PURPOSE, AND THE FUNCTION OF BUTTONS

The sun has retreated behind the clouds, blanketing the streets in their usual grey pallor. It feels tighter here. The crowds no longer thrum with life, everyone eager to retire to their beds. I hold my breath around the hacking, fighting the urge to press my sleeve to my face and keep the bad air out.

Now, all there is to do is wait. Through my headache and churning stomach, I wonder if risking my life over this case is worth it.

The woman leading me fearlessly through the crowd sure seems to think so.

My worries fade when we turn onto a different street—the Limehouse Causeway. The grey and glum buildings are peppered with vibrant red and green shop signs, some with striking characters painted in gold. Alleyways narrow, as do the buildings that pave the cobblestone road. Laundry lines hang from window to window, their garments fluttering like flags in the breeze. From one of the second-floor windows, the aroma of stewing fish intertwines pleasantly with the scent of brine.

We must be near the docks. My stomach lurches again. *Merde*, I'm starving.

Annie slows to a halt in front of a shop with Chinese lettering painted above the first-floor window, which is slightly fogged. An array of glass bottles and jars are visible just inside.

"Wait out here, okay?"

I nod, but a weathered yet sharp voice snaps from within, causing the both of us to jump.

"Bring him!"

Annie turns red and gives me a reassuring smile, the first she's offered me since our meeting. She beckons me in and vanishes between two towering cupboards; I try my hardest to follow, fearful of upsetting any of the hundreds of ingredient bottles, or the mysterious source of the rasping voice.

We're engulfed by the rich aromas of more anise, maybe something like fresh satsumas, and whatever else is ground up in these jars.

The array of cupboards opens up into a back room rainbowed in the same shade of brilliant red, silvers, bronzes, and gold dappled with green. Red is evidently significant here, but all it reminds me of is the woman hacking blood into her napkin.

"Amah, this is Jacques." Annie sounds flustered. "Jacques, this is my grandmother, Joy. And this is her spice shop."

Spice shop seems too inadequate a term for the array of bottles and sachets that surround me.

As I emerge from between the shelves, she's hugging what appears to be a mound of shawls, but when she pulls back, there's a tiny woman wrapped in fabric there.

Amah smiles warmly, but once her eyes fall upon me— probably my pallor—they widen. "What did you do?" The old woman's accented voice is sharp.

I freeze, even if the question is for her granddaughter.

"You told me to bring him in." Annie begins to fidget with her collar, loosening it. The power shift in the room is palpable.

"Good evening," I offer, stepping forward. "It's a pleasure to meet you." I'd like to shake her hand, but think better of it.

Amah frowns at Annie, already moving about the room— away from me. "Is he yours?"

"Yes. I mean, no, he's a work acquaintance."

Amah points at a round wooden table in the corner, where a glass aquarium sits in the middle, just big enough for two. "Come," she directs me. "You look hungry."

"No," Annie insists as I shake my head despite my hunger. "We need a favor."

"I'm not talking to you," her grandmother snaps. Her assessing eyes lock onto me, narrowing distrustfully. The apple does not fall far from its tree here. "Sit."

I saunter across the room and sit at the table, where a pair of goldfish peek out at me from the reeds.

"Jacques was caught in the rain on his walk home from work last night," Annie continues. "Might you have anything for him? To ensure he stays well, or anything that develops remains mild. He's afraid a cough will develop."

"Medicine."

As Annie nods, her grandmother studies me.

Grunting, Amah opens and disappears into the door behind her, and I'm immediately hit with the aromas of garlic, onion, and ginger before it slams shut. My stomach growls so loudly, I'm sure Annie can hear it.

But she's busy exhaling, removing her gloves with her teeth and offering nothing consoling, or even insulting. Her heels remain grounded across the room, and I wonder if she's regretting her decision of bringing me home. Or thinking about those shears in her pocket.

The door swings open, and Amah returns with two steaming bowls. She places them down, one before me and the other, at the vacant chair. Annie doesn't wait for Amah to beckon her over, and she's sitting on my right when the old woman holds her hand out to me expectantly.

I'm about to reach for the coins in my pocket, when she roughly grabs my left palm.

"Amah!"

"*Quiet*, Annabelle." Amah positions herself over my palm and peers closely at it. There's far more strength in her weathered hands than appearance suggests. She lets go and turns my face this way and that in her pincer-like grip. The lines at her mouth vanish beneath a tight, unreadable smile.

Annie blows on a spoonful of steaming broth, the rising scents of anise and spring onion doing little to mask her discomfort. "What is it?"

Amah appears satisfied as she releases me, but the fact that Annie has to ask unnerves me. She's read something in her grandmother's expression.

"There are certain illnesses that don't just weaken the body, but stir up whatever's waiting underneath. Medicine will not help what is becoming." The old woman gestures to the broth. "But filling the belly might slow it."

Without further explanation, she turns away and disappears into the front of the shop, her slippers whispering against the floorboards.

Don't get me wrong—Annie is a mad genius for suggesting I fall ill, then seek early treatment at her grandmother's to prevent the worst of it before going to the infirmary. I'll look back upon this eve in impressed fondness one day when the rush of blood to my face doesn't worsen the pain in my head.

"Looks like I caught it."

"Eat," is all Annie says, scraping around her bowl. She's

determined to appear unconcerned, and I can't tell if it's for her benefit or mine. "Hunger won't do you any good. Amah's food is also medicine, especially *jūk*. It's what she says all the time."

She is right, after all. The broth is delicious, thickened with glutinous rice and thinly sliced ginger. Palpable warmth begins to spread throughout my body. It's unlike anything I've ever had.

The last mouthful leaves a trace of lingering heat down my throat, and I feel suddenly sluggish. The ache behind my eyes has dulled.

I blink at the fish. They blink back.

My bowl's empty. Amah is gone. The shop is warm, and its scents lull me against the back of my chair.

Annie's still beside me, pushing the dregs of ginger around her bowl, though I'm not sure she's eaten anything for minutes. She sneaks glances at me from behind a wave of hair, backlit in the last rays of apricot dusk filtering through the shelves. Her lips part, like she might say something.

Instead, there's the scrape of wood. A chair moving, a breath too close to my shoulder, and the scent of jasmine. "Jacques?"

Wet fabric clings to my spine and I suddenly realize I'm sweating—drenched, as if I'd been running. I need to stand, to rouse myself, but my limbs are much too heavy to lift.

"You're burning," she utters, and I feel the back of her fingers against my forehead.

"I'm just tired," I say, or try to say, but the words slur at the edges. The room is tilting. There's a distant clatter… then, I'm moving.

There are arms under mine, my own feet barely supporting my weight. Wool against my thin shirt—a hallway, then a narrow stair.

Her breath hitches, soft curses in Chinese. My head rolls against her shoulder before everything folds inward.

FOR THE FIRST time in over thirty days, my sleep is not impeded by nightmares of my father vomiting blood as the men who swarm us stab him repeatedly with a wooden bayonet. *Run*, he gargles, just before I wake up.

But the world here is dim, and Annie the seamstress is on my lips, my tongue, my fingers. On my still-pounding teeth, although the pain in my temples has been since replaced by a dull headache.

"I can smell you," I groan. "Everywhere." What an odd thing to say, yet it is the first thing that escapes my mouth.

I might've dreamt it. Hopefully that was the case.

"Well, you *have* been sleeping in my bed."

My eyes open, and I turn on my side to feel for her.

Annie isn't there, but at the foot of the bed I'm cocooned upon, perched on what appears to be a large trunk. Her coat hangs on the rack near the door in the corner of the room. A bundle of fabric is on her lap, and her tiny fingers work fluidly with a needle and thread. There's a mirror to her right, propped diagonally from the corner and looking into the room.

"How long?" I peer out the window behind me. It's dark, and the lamps are on, but the streets aren't nearly as empty as I'd expect them to be closer to midnight.

"Three hours."

I sit up, and it's at this moment I realize I'm shirtless. "What are you doing?"

"You asked for pants earlier in the shop. Here they are."

I run my hand across my bare torso, no longer wet or fevered. I'm wearing only my drawers beneath the thick blanket, which I pull further up to keep myself decent as I shrink back into her pillows.

"Don't worry. Amah took care of you."

"How comforting."

"You fell asleep in your bowl of *jūk*." She withholds a laugh. "Spilt half of it all over your crotch."

"I finished the bowl. It was delicious."

"No, you had a few bites then passed out."

I rub my eyes, not about to argue. If she's right, it's probably why I'm still starving. Despite the acid eating my stomach, I feel rejuvenated by the sleep. Strong.

Annie brings the thread to her mouth and snaps it between her teeth. "Here." She stands. "Get up."

I can already tell by the ghost of her form beneath her clothes, and the pair of black trousers she holds up—ones that aren't my own—that this is a bad idea. I scramble for an excuse.

Anything other than, *I refuse to stand before you because I am ragingly stiff in this loose pair of undergarments.*

But Annie respects my wishes and drapes the pants over my chest. "They were my uncle's. He and my mother died a few years ago in a carriage incident." She clears her throat, as if it embarrasses her to overshare. "They were large for you, so I made some light adjustments while you slept."

"Thank you," I mutter. She's beautiful. Kind. Smart. Terrifying, of course—but generous. "This isn't the pair he… he erm—"

Annie dissolves into a fit of laughter, already turning for the door. The richness of her voice and the very sound of her joy send me into stark panic. "They're new, I don't think he'd ever worn them." Her hand goes for the knob, but an unsure sound forms at the back of my throat.

"You don't have to go. Not if you don't want to."

Her fingers linger on the doorknob. But she doesn't leave.

When her back is to me, I swing my legs from the bed and pad barefoot to the floor-length mirror, where my shoes and socks are placed at the end of the bed.

I don't exactly know what is in the fabric she's stitched, but it smells faintly of her, too. Of spice, or herbs… maybe soap and sweat, but most certainly something iron-rich beneath it all.

Desperate to hide my erection, I tug the trousers on; they're still warm from her lap, and fall perfectly at my waist. Not too tight, but fitted. They're not loose enough to conceal my cock, however, but there's not much I can do about that. I smooth the material—her work is precise, as if made by someone who knows my body. I glance into the mirror as my fingers fumble with the buttons, too busy watching the curve of her spine reflected as she lingers at the door, swaying slightly.

"I don't think I've ever had a pair of trousers fit this way," I say, playful accusation lacing my tone. "They're shaped to me."

"I've been doing this for a long time. Sewing tears in my own dolls since I was a child. I'm good at estimating," she murmurs without turning. "I don't even have to touch a client to know."

Shame.

I reach for my undershirt folded on the wide dresser to the left of the trunk, but then I hesitate, my eyes glued to the mirror.

I must have sweated well throughout my slumber; my chest is defined, the skin over my sternum, smooth. The veins along my collarbone are darker than I remember, like ink under the thinnest parchment. When I drag a hand across my ribs, I expect the tenderness from fever and the nausea to return. Instead, my flesh is mild, nothing other than the persistent growl of my belly plaguing me. Even the fine golden hairs at my forearms seem to catch the lamplight in ways they shouldn't.

When I look up, Annie is watching me in the mirror. As soon as I make eye contact, she makes her way over, holding my gaze the entire time. When she reaches me, she stands at my side and lifts her fingers to the waistband of my trousers. They linger there, ghosting along the stitch line at my hip. Her gaze then flickers down, assessing as she takes in the cut below my navel.

I shudder, rebuking the illness—the strange spirit, whatever it may be—that urges me to curl my arms around her.

"I did these too quickly," she says decidedly. "I may need to take them in again."

"How long?" I ask, desperate for a distraction.

Her eyes snap up, no longer suspicious, but transfixed at the rasp in my voice. The firelight sets them aglow. "What?"

Annie's long, thick lashes bat at me—God, she's close enough to devour—and my own question nearly escapes me. "Your mother. How long ago did she die?"

"Oh. Thirteen years ago."

"And this was here?"

Her face scrunches before she scowls. "This is your way of gauging where I'm from. What I'm *doing* here."

My heart skips a horrid beat. "No, I—"

"My grandfather Shing was a dock laborer out of Guangdong for years before work became unstable. The British firms had slowly shifted their control onto the dock operations, and he was eventually released. Months passed before he was approached to be a translator." Annie's eyes twinkle, unseeing in the lamplight. "His employer promised he'd work abroad for a few months, making a short stop in England before being dropped off in Singapore, where there were better chances for steady positions. Lucrative wages.

So, he, Amah, my mother, and my uncle left their home in hopes of a better one."

"Your family never made it to Singapore."

"My grandfather was so eager to give them a better life, no one questioned the lack of a formal document or contract. Not that it would have mattered." Her laugh is empty before she clears her throat, as if rehearsed to distance herself from the weight of a past she never lived. "They got off the ship here at the docklands when my mother needed cough medicine, and were never allowed back on."

It's unfathomable. Detestable. "I'm so sorry, Annie."

"It's fine," she replies too quickly. "It's not mine to carry."

But it's obvious she does.

"And how old are you?" My voice is unintentionally rough.

"I'll be thirty-one in November." Annie flinches belatedly at my direct questioning in regard to her, as if she's shocked she'd answered so quickly.

"You were young when you lost your mother. And you care for your grandmother here?"

"The shop owners offered me my mother's position when she died and we'd run out of wages. I go to work in the early mornings to help them set up and then come home to her." She doesn't look upset, nor ungrateful. Just pensive, as if she's wondering where the years have gone. As if she's pondered her next step many nights before, yet didn't quite know how to proceed.

"Alone?" My questioning is far too forward, but I cannot help myself. It is the only thing I can do to keep myself from staring unabashedly at the swell of her full bottom lip, which she bites in anticipation. Her fingers sit painstakingly still, a brush away from the dick I cannot help but think with.

Except, it's not even that. What I feel here is much more than that.

And, to my relief, Annie Castro-Tan is far, far smarter.

"If you're so concerned for my safety, you'd know admitting to a strange man that I live alone with my grandmother is the worst possible thing I could do."

I crane my neck down at her. "Worse than inviting that strange man into your home?" Her mouth twists. "Worse than bringing him into your room? Inviting him to sleep in your bed?"

"Inviting you into my bed, and plopping you there because the other rooms are occupied with my dead relatives' belongings are two very different things."

"Having him undress for you?"

"You haven't asked me about a father," she challenges. "My dead grandfather." Her fingers then curl around to the front of my waistband, her nails slipping *into* it—not loosening or measuring anything. Annie's testing the fabric between us. "What is it you're asking me, Jacques?"

I exhale, unsteady. Her knuckles graze my skin as they sink deeper, and I feel the contact a bit too sharply, as though my nerves are tuned too finely. I don't move, not because I can't, but because I can't trust myself to. My skin flushes and prickles, like something is trying to break outward as my body awaits a command it hasn't yet received.

As if realizing what she's doing, she looks up, and whatever she sees in my expression makes her breath hitch.

Still, she steps closer. *Quelle petite sotte.*

The corner of Annie's mouth lifts, and she teeters on her toes until her breath ghosts my jaw. I can just about taste her, feel her running through my fingers. "You understand that I am sick, don't you? That I've caught whatever ails this town?"

Annie just laughs. "And I walk amongst them every day. Chat with them. Work with them. The dying are next door to our shop. It's only a matter of time."

She shouldn't think that way. The mere thought of any

harm coming to her grips me in rage. The thought of being responsible for it sends anguish ripping through my chest.

Swallowing, I step back. I've forgotten myself. My honor, my manners.

"I should leave," I manage, but then one of her hands goes to my face, her thumb repeatedly stroking my tensed jaw until it loosens.

"You don't want to."

I don't. I don't, because she's made me forget why I came here, the things I'm running from and the case I'm meant to be solving. She's made me forget the blood on the streets and the ghosts in my lungs, and because there's something in her —stubborn, and grieving, and warm—that calls out to something deep in me.

She's lost, too. Her uncle, her mother. She knows the pain of a family broken disassembled into nothing but empty rooms and folded clothes collecting dust.

I've carried absence like a second skin; my mother's prayers the night before she left, years before I'd even begun my training. The gaping hole she left in our home. My father's death that feels like a lifetime ago... showing up repeatedly to the Commissaire, begging the police there for answers. A simple mugging, or attempted robbery, is how they classified it. The investigation stalled once they discovered it was the brilliant private detective who often made their jobs more difficult with his unconventional methods and penchant for empathy.

My father's name became well known; he'd submerged himself in his craft of giving people answers. Closure over arrests. And no one did the same for him.

I'd never anticipated how deafening loss could be until the day it echoed through my bones, ravaging me from the inside out.

But Annie understands this feeling. As strong-willed as

she is, she's as marked by grief as I am. This type of loneliness doesn't fade. Maybe that's why I'm drawn to her, because there's a reflection there. I'm sure there are days she's collapsed upon this very floor like I have.

What would it take to be the one who caught her then?

"No," I croak, barely audible.

"Then say that instead."

And I do. Except, I say it in the form of her name, and bend to kiss her like I'm starving.

Because I am.

Her palm slides down the front of my trousers the tender moment her tongue meets mine. She wraps her hands around my girth, gasping and smiling into my mouth as I lift her. She's not a short woman, broad-shouldered with unbelievable curves under her loose clothing that I can now feel, but she weighs next to nothing with all of the adrenaline slamming through me.

"My dresser," she says feverishly, wrapping her legs around me. I hesitate—there are things there, some of her belongings, but her voice is thick her want. "You wouldn't care if I offered you to taste me."

At this, I am not only a man starved, but parched. Without another word, I turn and sit her upon it, and she sweeps her hands across the top to make room, knocking a cup and several compacts off. Annie then unbuttons the top of her blouse—three down, just enough to bare her cleavage, when three more would have removed the garment altogether.

Tu oses me braver ainsi. At this moment, her very existence is a provocation.

I press my lips to the tops of her breasts, groaning against the plump veins I can't help but notice as my hand slips beneath her skirts.

She stills, watching in fascination as I sink to my knees

and find her entrance; her lips part, and she gasps when I splay her slick arousal between my fingers, thumbing her sensitive clitoris. I swallow, gauging her reaction, waiting for her nod before I bring my mouth to her cunt.

It comes quickly. Shudderingly. "Please," she mouths.

Annie. She tastes even better than she smells. Warm, floral, and sweet. But when my fingers enter her gently, my other hand finding purchase in the flesh of her thighs as I tongue her... Her head falls back, exposing her throat.

She rocks her hips forward and palms her breast as I continue, my breath hot and shallow against her.

I glance up to enjoy the view, and immediately regret it.

My mind instantly blanks. I'm thrusting into her, feeling her muscles—her *blood*—pulse and coil around me, but all I see are the blue-green roadmaps and rivers dancing across her beautiful skin—the calligraphy inevitably leading me to a most unholy oblivion.

I'll try it, I tell myself. Feel my lips against her pulse and stop there... because, what else would I do?

I'm pulled from my thoughts when she squirms against my face. I rise over her, and she whimpers in surprise when I flatten my tongue into the hollow of her neck. Unaware of the strange hungers festering inside me, Annie pulls me closer, her nails digging into my arms.

Unthinking, I drag my tongue slowly up the side of her throat to her earlobe.

"Jacques," she moans.

It's at this moment, I come to understand that this is the danger in her—of this. She has no idea I am overcome with the sudden urge to grip her by the throat and have her take my cock. No idea my urges grow *beyond* that—that I'd like to nothing else but to claim her and paint her in burgundy.

In wine, right? I blink rapidly. *Jam? Figs?*

I've straightened in alarm, but she lurches toward me, her

throat rising toward my mouth hung open in self-disgust. I jerk away from her.

"Jacques?" Annie says again, this time in alarm. Her face is deliciously flushed. "What's wrong?"

"I—" I swipe my arm against my mouth, my tongue, panting hard. I taste iron—an alarming sweetness on my tongue. "Nothing," I rasp, easing out of her and quickly planting my lips upon her forehead. "It's nothing."

A lie, and a poor one at that. She takes both sides of my face between her palms. "You're trembling, you know."

"So are you."

"Yes, but I hide it better."

That, she does. Overcome with need, I reach for her waist, and she meets me where I stand. She slides off the dresser and kisses me harder, desperately, as if she needs this, too. Needs me to enter her, fill her. Bleed her dry.

Whatever the fuck is wrong with me roars to life when she falls against me. I drown in her, her nails sliding up my bare back. My hips press back into hers, and I feel the very moment she is undone, her whole being coming alive in heat and friction.

I spin her, just before we crash backward onto her bed.

I follow Annie down like I've done it a thousand times before—like we have a lifetime to go. My hands slip under her skirts again, and her legs open eagerly beneath me. I remove her undergarments and slide my own trousers down —carefully, so as not to ruin all of her hard work—and hover over her.

Annie slips me out of my pants before I'm done, fisting me. Her eyes widen in delight as I begin to thrust slowly.

"Do you like it when I fuck your hand, Annabelle?"

She only manages a nod.

My heart is thrumming, and I swear I can feel her pulse as much as I imagine tasting it. But my blunt, throbbing teeth would fuck her throat up—of that much I'm aware, even in my state of delirium.

Yes. That's what it is. And I might've doomed Annie to it, too.

The feeling of my head against her pussy yanks me from my worried reverie; she's angled me down, guiding me.

I think I'm about to come the moment I sheathe myself and the sound of her shallow panting invades my senses— but there's slight resistance there. I frown, but she arches toward me hungrily, seeking friction, so I bring my mouth to hers and give it to her.

Annie lets out a muffled gasp as my cock eases in, and I'm just halfway in when I feel her stiffen beneath me.

Freezing, I slowly pull myself out to see myself covered in a layer of her arousal, and—

And… My eyes go entirely black.

I wasn't thinking—haven't *been* thinking. She's unmarried, unspoken for. Cares for her grandmother. I myself haven't been with anyone for years. Not this way.

She watches my face contort in realization, and her cheeks are suddenly dusted in rose. "I didn't think it mattered. I told you about myself. What I do here. I don't know what you were expecting."

When I don't reply—I'm unable in the moment, feeling the alarming urge to open and snap my jaws shut—she moves to sit up.

"It *doesn't* matter." I fix the dumbfounded expression I'm wearing and bring her hand to my mouth, speak against her knuckles, my lips lingering longer than they should as I try my hardest not to glance down at the glistening red covering me. "And I wasn't expecting anything from you. I promise."

Annie hesitates, watching me closely, reading too much in the pause before I flip and kiss her inner wrist, as if she's waiting for me to regret this. Regret *her*. To pull back or change my mind.

I don't.

"You think your inexperience is something I mind?" I murmur, dragging my gaze up to meet hers. "*Mon cœur*, it only makes this more precious."

"I am not inexperienced," she growls softly, her guard giving way to something deeper, more profound than annoyance. "I've been pleasured before. And I've brought myself to it. But I've tended to my grandmother since I was seventeen, not out of duty alone. I care for her. She is my only family here." Annie's face is bright red. "One doesn't easily come and go from such a life, you see. It leaves little room for leisure or introductions, let alone attachments."

"You've given so much of yourself without asking for anything in return. I'm sure your grandmother is grateful, and the people who truly matter will see how special that is. They will wait if they must. If this is your first time, then I'd be honored to be the one to make you feel safe in it. Wanted. And, if not…" I offer her a smile I hope is consoling rather than hungry. "I have time. Lots of it."

"Health and fortune on your side, granting," she adds.

I laugh unexpectedly, but the distrust in Annie's eyes starts to return. And for good reason.

I've gripped myself over her. Her noticing, watching me start to pump my cock with her come and blood, is sickening, yet I don't think I've ever been more hard. There is something wholly, utterly wrong with me tonight, and I cannot help it.

Annie cups my hand in hers and begins to move our fingers together, up and down my shaft, mesmerized. "You enjoy this, don't you?"

"Yes," I admit, low in my throat.

"Revolting," she breathes. But excitement swallows her pupils whole. "What else do you like?"

It has been so long, I don't remember what I like outside of having the company of a beautiful woman in my bed. I don't even know if I've had the time or opportunity to explore what I enjoy, but of two things I'm certain—that I've never been graced by such a lethal presence before, and that the urges I feel tonight have never once plagued me.

Restraint altogether has eluded me since the moment I stepped into Lewis & Allenby's. Stepped onto the dock, really.

I'm unable to formulate words as she guides my hand up, and down, licking her lips.

"Show me," Annie mouths.

Fuck. I rise over her, and this time my kiss is fierce and demanding. Her body responds immediately; Annie's fingers go to the remainder of her blouse buttons.

I catch her hand at her front. "You're always the one dressing others. Undressing them, making them feel their best. Allow me do to that for you."

There's reluctance there, but she obliges as I begin removing her clothes, lace by lace. Layer by layer. When I peel her chemise away, my mouth goes dry. She is exquisite…

And *distracted*, gripping me and canting my head toward her with one hand. It is I who shudders when she guides me past her ridden up skirt. I groan and lean into her, cupping her full breasts with one hand, teasing a peaked nipple with my tongue and teeth.

When I pull away, Annie looks up at me, her eyes sultry and dark, framed by wisps of lashes that beckon my soul; she sucks the blood off of her middle and ring fingers as I slowly enter her.

I'm about to lose myself, yet feel at home at the same time.

My hand travels from her breast, up the side of her throat as I stroke her, gently at first, with what little restraint I can manage. My fingers settle upon her neck, just below her jaw.

Her eyes widen.

"Does this scare you?" I whisper.

She doesn't answer at first, but her entire face and chest flush, blooming in heat and blood. I need to be near it. Taste it.

I bend to her throat—but there's the cold bite of metal against my ear. In my periphery, the pair of shears hovers inches from my face. I don't move, my pace gradually slowing, but not out of fear.

"You think I'm the one who should be scared?" she asks, holding the point perpendicular to my throat.

I swallow, and the movement presses the metal against my skin. Her eyes wield a strange hunger of her own; she's not bluffing, not entirely. Annie waits patiently as I continue to fuck her—panting, almost as if she's determined to see me flinch. Almost as if she wants me to prove I'm not just another man who will entertain her until she draws blood, or whatever it is she's experienced to make her arm herself this way.

But I don't. Instead, I curl my hand around the side of her throat, reaching under, not to grip or threaten, but to cradle her. Remind her that I'm still here. Still a man amidst the want and delirium, and… and hunger. Still hers.

Stabbing me—or whatever it is she plans to do—can wait. I'm not finished with her.

I bring my mouth to hers; that seems to be okay. She kisses me back hungrily, and my thrusts grow deeper, longer as she arches into me. Whimpering against my lips, Annie stretches and crests over my cock, and I swallow the sound. With one particularly rough thrust, the shears fall to the mattress. She's scrabbling at my back, scratching and likely drawing blood, but I don't care.

All I can think about is hers.

And we… *I* haven't even considered protection. Surely her poor grandmother can hear the bed creaking and my grunting like some poor beast.

"Annie," I pant against her cheek, grazing my teeth along her ear. "I'm going to come. Where do you want it?"

What the fuck did I mean, *Where do you want it?* What was I *doing?*

Once I start coughing, once the fever returns for good, the port authorities would bar me from entry back to Paris. I'd have to make a full recovery here.

But… I was never going to return to France, was I? I'd known that when I accepted the summons and stuffed nearly every piece of clothing from my *appartement* in Saint-Germain into two luggages.

I would not return to my home ill, not with everything behind me. At the very least, not without her.

I freeze. *Does she know that?*

Fighting these monstrous urges of lust and craving the companionship I most definitely do not deserve, I move to pull out of her—but Annie's fingers find my throat, squeeze, and yank me closer. I snarl, my hand flying warningly to her wrist. But I don't dare remove it.

"Come for me, Jacques," she begs, her voice like honey. "Wherever you want to."

That's all I need to hear from her. I buck, groaning against her collarbone, our sweat and sex mixing in the heat of the late September night, tempered by the gentle breeze fluttering the curtain's edge across the top of Annie's head.

I ease myself out of her, and she directs me to a neat pile of laundry in a basket under her bed. I clean her gently— she's no longer bleeding—and just when I tug my drawers on and find her a nightgown from her drawers, a slow, winding melody floats up from the cracked window.

Annie finishes tugging the sheer gown over her head and crawls over her bed to peer out the window. We both glance down to spot a lone fiddler in the street, entertaining some of the night crowd.

"At this hour," I comment, my forehead refreshingly cool against the windowpane. I'm not grumbling; the tune is pleasantly morose, somewhere between a waltz and a dirge. One I'd find out of place for a street entertainer.

But tonight, as the stars hold their breath and these strange hungers subside, it's fitting.

Beside me, Annie's on her hands and knees humming, her eyelids heavy with sleep. But she doesn't cocoon herself in the duvet under us. Instead, she shuffles off the bed.

Like a man possessed, I follow.

"Dance with me," she murmurs, the ghost of her gown swirling around her calves, the waves of her hair brushing her shoulderblades.

And so, I do. Barefoot on the worn floorboards, half-dressed and unguarded, swaying in the glow of a flickering oil lamp and the soft silver spilling in from the window. Her cheek rests against my chest, my chin upon her head as I cradle her. I press a tender kiss into her hair, and know immediately that this single night, in all of its quiet magic, is not enough.

"Jacques?" Annie says, after we've been swaying for a while. Minutes or an hour is anybody's guess.

"Annabelle?"

She speaks without craning her head up. "Take what medicine Amah gives you tomorrow, and forget Beecham's Infirmary, okay?"

The infirmary is the very reason I'm here, and it wouldn't look very good on my resume if I abandoned the case, but it had happened on occasion. I was contracted, and didn't work *for* the police here. I'd never work for them. I'd find other jobs eventually… a different line of work entirely. Not that I'd be in any particular hurry. There are certain lingering benefits to having once belonged to a family like mine.

"Do you mean, pursue it later?" I ask.

"Forget it altogether."

I pull back; her expression is hesitant, as if she understands the weight of what she's asking. I only smile and twirl her. "And? What do you propose we do instead?"

Annie ducks under my arm. "Fresh air and some sunlight would be good for you. There's a place near the old cathedral. St Paul's. It's quiet, all stone and shrubbery. Mom and I used to go there when I was little."

"A church?"

"The *husk* of one. Moss. Tombstones. There's a difference."

I don't need further convincing. I hum against her, and we continue dancing until after the fiddler has retired. She's cradled in the crook of my arm, and we lay there side by side, listening to the sounds of the street.

Annie is radiant in the lamplight, as if her skin is illuminated from within, and I find myself wondering how, after becoming so well acquainted with grief, I've managed to end up here. In this creature's arms, as she burns up with life. It feels suspiciously like reprieve, or a dream I won't survive.

CHAPTER 4

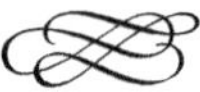

IN WHICH GOODBYE TASTES LIKE BLOOD AND THE STREETS OF LONDON WAIT WITH BATED BREATH

In the early hours of morning, a sense of foreboding lures me from the sweetest slumber. The room smells faintly of sweat and blood—and smoke, as if a tail of incense wafts somewhere downstairs. Outside, the early light has yet to press fully into the town, leaving everything dipped in dim blue.

Even Annie, curled next to me with her arm under her cheek, facing the window. Her hair is strewn across her face, stuck to her forehead in sweat, and I reach out to sweep it off.

But, as my hand ghosts her flushed skin, I hesitate, so as not to wake her. Because for a moment last night, I'd wholeheartedly believed her. Believed I could vanish into London's folds of chimney and cobblestone and disappear with her. That the past—the blood, the cases, my father, and the strange hungers stirring awake within my bones—could all be forgotten.

And I believe it now, until I sit up and a terrible chill ghosts my back. The blankets below me are *soaked*. It feels like I've dumped an entire kettle there. There's a slight ache to my joints, a distant throb in my gums; other than that, I don't feel anything out of the ordinary, otherwise.

But under my sweat-slicked skin, the fever must be raging.

I glance down at Annie, truly worried I'd doomed her to the same fate. I'm about to touch her again—feel her, perhaps even rouse her and express my concerns—when there's a soft knock at the door.

Stumbling out of bed, I tug on my trousers, making enough noise to signal that *someone* was getting up to answer. I don my undershirt and run my hand though my hair, flattening it, trying to look anything like we'd made love last night—and pull the door open. Annie's grandmother stands at the threshold, wrapped in her shawls. In her gnarled, steady hands, is a small lacquered box.

"Good morning, Amah." I do a terrible job at forcing the sleep from my voice.

"For the blood," she says simply, holding the box out to me. She pops the lid back, revealing two bags stacked upon each other. "Not to feed it, but to cool it. *Guī bǎn, bái sháo,* and *dān shēn.*" Amah prods the one on top containing a coarse, light brown powder.

"To cool my blood," I repeat, aware of how idiotic I must sound. She is obviously well-versed in her area of medicine. "Anything to warm it?"

I half mean it as a joke, but Amah's eyes twinkle in the lamplight. She lifts that first bag up, and there's a second underneath. "This," she says, prodding the bottom bag. It looks like a paste of ground herbs. "To give you strength when the cold tries to break you. *Fùzǐ, Diānqié,* and Ginger Root. Balances the fire in your soul."

I know nothing of botany; of all the herbs named, I'm only familiar with last. In fact, I'd had my fair share of it last night in that delicious broth. But I trust her. I have no other choice.

Before I can accept them, I begin to feel the fever crawling like a snake beneath my skin. I make to retreat, fearful of the symptoms returning or worsening.

I want to run, to go back to Annie.

But Amah remains, expectantly studying me. "You came to this town for answers, didn't you? Beecham has them."

How could she have known? Annie must've explained everything to her.

"Amah," I say, every bit of reverence and worry I feel evident in my low voice. "My main concern is Annie. Has she… have I passed this onto her?"

"No. Anything she's dealing with is on the surface, a lingering heat that I can help cool here. I will care for her." Amah regards her snoring granddaughter from the doorway. "But what's inside you won't respond to medicine alone."

My stomach coils, my mouth dry. I nod, my fingers wrapping tightly around the two bundles.

"If you stay, you'll only delay what's already begun. If you do go…" Her gaze lifts to the window, and the waking town beyond. "You'll save her, and so many more."

I STAND at the edge of the bed and take one last look at her.

Annie lies tangled in the blankets, one arm draped across her ribs. She looks young like this. Softened, unguarded when she sleeps. The fever hasn't touched her face yet. Or maybe it has, and I just don't want to see it.

I want to stay. God, I do. But something deep within me needs to see this through, to get better for her. To find answers for the Wharncliffes. We'll have that day together at St Paul's, but for now, answers and a cure await me. I bend down, press my lips to her temple, and breathe her in. Jasmine, sin, and the sweet edge of blood.

"I'll come back for you. Even if I have to claw my way."

She stirs against me but doesn't wake.

I take one last look about the room, the weight of Amah's herbs solid in my pocket, and step into the hall. Amah is waiting by the stairwell, arms folded, shawl wrapped tight around her. She doesn't say anything. Just nods once, dutifully guarding her granddaughter's door.

I descend the stairs slowly, boots against wood the only sound in the entire house, every step pulling me further from the night I'd like to hold onto.

At the bottom, a long table holds the incense I'd smelled earlier, curls of smoke wafting undisturbed into the entryway like curled petals of chrysanthemum. Just when I creak the door open, there's a faint shuffling behind me.

It's Amah, descending the stairs. "Remember yourself, Jacques."

The morning is cold, the sun slow to rise though the London fog. My returning fever is the only thing keeping me warm in these empty streets. The world feels like it's paused here, a sepulchral spectre watching from the mist.

I turn and take Amah's extended hand, bow to press my lips to the back of it, and start walking. Each step forward is heavy, but I don't stop. Not this time.

CHAPTER 5

IN WHICH FILES ARE FOUND, TEETH ARE TAKEN AS TITHE, AND THE BODY MUST BE BROKEN TO REAP THE BLOOD

"Good day to you. Thank you." I wave to the driver that had appeared at the end of the square. He didn't say much, and it wasn't a long drive, but I'm grateful for the lift.

Lewis & Allenby's is closed, I notice, approaching the infirmary. Windows dim, curtains drawn. In fact, most of the businesses on the empty block seem to be.

I've forgotten it's Sunday. A day for the Sabbath—and Beecham's reckoning.

I'm prepared to knock repeatedly, announce my presence, or try and shoulder my way in. But the door swings inward almost as soon as I grip the knob.

Inside, intake is uneventful. Dull, almost. The receiving room is bare. Brand new wooden floors that are so pristine they're nearly reflective. The walls, which are not new, are covered in faded lime-green paint, and naked. There's nothing here, save for two chairs against a wall, another door, and a small window through which they take my information.

The old woman in the grey gown and cap stares at me

boredly above the surgeon's mask stuck to her mouth, and seems to be on the brink of turning me away until I pull out my business card for identification. I consider pulling out my letter of authority to work in London from the commissioner, but purposefully decide against that, and keep it in my back pocket.

I am a patient here, first and foremost. A fly on the wall.

The intake nurse disappears into the doorway behind her. It's not long before the door to my left swings open, and I'm brought into triage.

Four nurses seems excessive, but they're kind enough to walk ahead of me, and chat amongst themselves through their masks about the weather, before offering me a cup of water, which I gratefully accept but slosh into a plant pot as we round a corner. We enter a spacious hallway lined with doors, forking off to the right and left at the end. A short line of patients in monochrome robes made of coarse flannel offer feeble, tight-lipped smiles as we pass. At the rear is a young man, maybe even younger than me, in a wheelchair pushed by an attendant. As he passes, I can see there's a crude gash on his shin, open and uncovered; I wasn't trying to stare, but the swarm of buzzing flies is deafening in my right ear. Part of his bone is visible toward the front, where flies, gnats, and a cluster of squirming maggots make their home. Some of the flying insects have stuck to the pus leaking down his leg.

I should've stopped there and asked his name, what he was being seen for—evidently *not* his weeping wound—and hauled him out to a real hospital.

Instead, I stumble into the wall lost for words. I exaggerate a few coughs to mask my retching, which must work, because one of the nurses grips my shoulders and steers me into the first room around the left corner.

They attempt to robe me right away, grabbing at my

waistcoat and trousers, but I protest, unsettled. They're strong, and continue as if they hadn't heard me; I'm so taken aback by this, it takes me a few tries—maybe they speak another language—but I shout with everything in my arsenal. English, French, Latin, Occitan, Spanish…even my grandmother's native tongue of Breton. Still, they tug at me until I secure two of their wrists in one hand and shove a finger in the others' faces.

"I am fevered," I snarl gently, as if they don't see my undershirt stuck to my armpits, or the sweat curling and sticking my hair to my forehead. "I don't need to remove my clothes. I *need* to speak to Beecham."

They exchange glances, whispering, but not uttering a word directly to me. Their eyes are steeled above their masks. One nods, and they let me go. It is only then that they place the robe down on the counter and file out, one by one.

"The doctor will see you shortly," is all that is uttered to me by the last, before the door slams shut.

A wave of panic crests over me; I immediately go to follow them, but the door is locked. The knob doesn't even wiggle, there's no movement when I try with all my might, as if it's jammed or blocked, or deadbolted from the outside.

I drop to my knees and peer through the slim space underneath.

Heels. Two of them, right up against the door. Someone's leaning against it.

Why are they like this—why are those nurses so *strong*? And not in the way that would make me suspect they'd done rigorous strength training, or were naturally burly, or simply accustomed to unruly patients… but, strong in the way where no force on earth budged them.

Breathing hard, I retreat. They can't see me like this, I can't let the doctors see me like this. An animal trying to escape. They'll keep me here, dismiss me as a madman. If the boy in the wheelchair was any standard to go by, not even taking poor Alma into account, this place needs to be shut down and investigated immediately by someone with considerably greater authority than I.

My head has begun to throb again, my stomach painfully acidic.

Through the commotion, I haven't even noticed the two chairs behind me. One for the patient, large and with a long back, with an array of mechanical contraptions attached to the side—probably to recline it. The other, a simple chair for the doctor. Shelves and cabinets line the back, but unlike Amah's shop, they're barren, or at least the shelves are.

I might as well make use of my time to snoop. I tread across the room and proceed to open them, left to right. The first holds gauzes and what I presume to be sterilizing liquid. The second is stacked with blocks of sharp-smelling carbolic soap next to a jarful of long, metal instruments submerged in alcohol. It is what's in the third cabinet that catches my eye.

A lone filing tin.

London, it's labeled. He must move offices often. *I wonder why*.

I take it down onto the counter, open it, and begin fingering through the documents. The first thing I see are names classified by alphabet.

I sort through all of them, making quick work of his patients' surnames. Despite Beecham's Infirmary existing here for little under a month according to Annie, there are dozens of files. They must be saturated; it's no wonder his patients are in such poor condition.

"Alma Wharncliffe," I mouth, flicking through the files. I stop to further loosen the ribbon at my collar; God, I'm burning up.

Look at me, dripping in sweat, trapped like some rabid animal. Scrounging through medical files and swallowing bile on the cusp of autumn. I should be boarding a ship right now, planning to show Annie and Amah the countryside.

I reach into my pocket and pull out the bags. *Which one did she mention does the cooling again?* The powder, I hope.

I place the dark paste back into my pocket and tear open the remaining bag with my teeth. Holding my nose, I empty the pouch into my mouth and chew. Even through my held breath, I can taste it. Briney, and sharp. I throw up in my mouth and force myself to swallow it again.

Charles better never thumb his fucking nose at me again.

Shuddering, I return to the documents. *Ashcombe. Bennett. Blackwood. Clarke. Davies. Deverill. Fletcher. Hollingsworth. Mason. Penhaligon. Turner.*

"Wharn…"

My fingers freeze on a file that sticks to my thumb in the humidity. *Val—*

I yank it out.

ETIENNE VALMONT. #003

There are notes written, much too neat and meticulous for a physician.

V-Series

Subject: Etienne Valmont

Notes: Failed integration.

Traits: Son of Sir Gaspard Austol Valmont, M.D.. High empathy, low submission. Failed transition. Subject escaped facility. Unknown fertility anomaly passed??? <u>Termination recommended</u>. Observation taken. Monitor bloodline, reacquire progeny if identified.

Risk: Medium.

I STARE at the date at the bottom. *November 1815, London.*

There's a scrawled set of initials in red ink over "Termination recommended."—A.B.

My mouth is dry. I fold and place the sheet in an empty pocket and, hands shaking with desperation and rage, return to the tin. Just to be sure…

I tug out the next and last *Valmont* entry.

JACQUES VALMONT #**383**

Series: Unknown.

Subject: Jacques Valmont

<u>Status: High priority anomaly</u>

Notes: External authorities informed. Presence requested (Patient #379 deployed). Do not initiate forced retrieval. Observe for pre-trigger manifestations; civilian contact has been briefed for observational support. Subject must remain unaware of her involvement.

Additional Notes: Patient inbound. Scheduled for extraction. Prepare restraints.

THE DOOR CLICKS, and I shove my record into my pocket, shut the tin, and place it back into the cabinet before swinging it shut—

Just as the door opens to reveal a middle-aged balding man in a white long coat, flanked by the four nurses who brought me in.

I stare at him from the corner like a trapped mongrel.

"Good morning, Jacques," he says, his accent indistinctly French, as if he'd been born there but spent most of his life among different tongues.

Red clouds my vision, and I don't even give them a chance. I bolt for the door—for him—but before I can wrap my hands around his windpipe, two of the nurses have me under the arms.

They lift me backward—off the floor when I start to fight—and into the patients' chair, where leather and metal restraints await me. It takes them all of five seconds to secure my wrists, thighs, and ankles, as if they've done this before, with subjects much bigger or stronger than I. There's some give at my torso and shoulders, so I twist, and I beg, and threaten, and snap my teeth at them.

I'm beyond tears. I want to tear his jugular out, slowly. Sinew by sinew.

The doctor only seems more pleased the more violent I grow.

"Hello, Monsieur Jacques," he sings, patting my head and keeping his weathered hands and wrists away from my mouth. His tone is unsettlingly pleasant. Familiar, even. He reaches into a drawer behind me and rummages through what sounds like metal, but I'm angled away and can't see. "I, am your uncle Beecham. Aloysius Ermengarde Beecham the Third. Long time no see."

"I've never seen you a day in my life."

He tilts his head in consideration. "True. I am a very good friend of your grandfather, though. Or, was. I'm sorry about his untimely demise. We fought alongside each other during the wars. I last visited him shortly before he succumbed to his illness, just after you were born. Told me to get the hell out of his manor after what I did to your father." A pensive smile ghosts his lips. "I couldn't imagine why. He was the very one who volunteered Etienne to become one of my first subjects."

How could this be? This man looked to be about my father's age, maybe a few years his senior. "What did you do to him?" I'm drooling in my anger, right on the verge of pissing myself.

"Etienne? That depends." His tone remains infuriatingly clinical. "Which time? When I tried to convert him? Or, when I had him terminated?"

Convert him to what? What was a V-Series? Why did he need to die?

A multitude of questions slam into me, but the only one that filters through is the one that tumbles out. "Did Annie know?"

He returns his gaze to me, and I'm suddenly afraid I've made a mistake in mentioning her. Despite what his notes might reveal, an unmistakable streak of rage overcomes me at the recognition in his eyes.

"Ah, Annie. You met the Tans, did you?"

"Je vais t'arracher les yeux et te les enfoncer dans la gorge." I speak to him in a language he well understands. "Answer me, you sick bastard!"

"There we are." Beecham stops rummaging. He scoots back with a large pair of rusted forceps in-hand.

I am effortlessly ignored as I shout for my release—for help, for God. For Annie.

The nurses stand in an eerie line around us, staring straight ahead, until Beecham mutters something to the nearest one. They swarm around me; one of them slams my head back to the chair and keeps it there, while the others lift the mechanical device attached to the side.

All the while, Beecham circles me with a notepad he's drawn out of his chest pocket, checking my pupils, my fingernails. He reaches down and palpates my abdomen. Without warning, his hand goes towards my mouth, which I instinctively lunge for, teeth bared in my blinding panic.

"Good," is the only word he mutters, yanking his fingers just in time. He scribbles more onto his notepad, muttering to himself. "Reflexes. Stamina. Everything I expected Etienne to become. The serum was already in you, shaping you.

Changing you through your inheritance of blood. I didn't think it could be passed down this way." He regards me in reverence. "Your body is extremely receptive. We've never seen it before. This is exactly what I wanted."

"Think *what* could be passed down this way?" No answer, still. I muster the will to coherently bellow the last thing on my mind. "I am a private inspector here on business. Alma Wharncliffe. You did the same to her as you did to my father. To everyone in those files, didn't you?"

He says something else in a foreign language I've never before heard to the nurses; they're waiting beside me with a large contraption in their hands. All of them move, except the one holding my forehead against the seat. She doesn't so much as budge as I strain and gasp and fight with everything in me.

The contraption is a cage, one for my head. The nurse holding me shifts out of the way as soon as they pull it over me, attaching it to the back of my seat with three clasps that clank shut. Wires and poles fit too tightly around my neck, crude points digging into my windpipe like a backward collar.

"Didn't you?" It's the last thing on my mind, but it's what I cling to. Anything to avoid thinking of my own fate, or never seeing Annie again. "*Look at me*—any of you! Her parents wanted closure, and all you gave them were her teeth." I buck, straining against the metal, nicking myself. Warm rivulets run down my collarbone. "I am a private investigator here on official business!"

"First and foremost, you are a patient in need." Unmoved, Beecham picks through his coat pocket and pulls on a mask. "Might you mean, her?" He points at the nurse on my far right. She's tall, but not as tall as the others. "Pull off your mask, dear. He's contained."

The nurse at my elbow does as she's told, pulling her

mask down over her chin. A girl of about ten smiles back at me, and I gasp, choking on bile.

Fangs—two glinting, metal pairs flanking her top middle teeth. The rest of her mouth is crusted in burgundy.

"You see, Jacques, *I* come from a noble house as well—though, not one as prominent as your grandfather's. Petite noblesse. Not as secure. Your legacy carries on, even without your father's blessing." Beecham spits onto the floor. "But I trained in medicine, and wanted to find a way to preserve the legacy of our name, too. There was a gentleman Gaspard and I met in a pub during our time as riflemen, who spoke of eternal life. Sold us a vial of what he called 'Immortality in a Bottle.' It was to be ingested, and eventually repurposed through patients."

I'd fall out of my chair laughing had I not been tied up.

"The Blood of the Undamned—half human, half undead. A bridge between species."

I start shaking my head, cutting myself deeper. This is preposterous.

"The arcane sort are cursed, according to him. Averse to sunlight, eyes ruby red after feeding. But *this* blood is superior. A brand of vampirism not found outside a single bloodline. None of that applies. And I am trying to recreate them."

"You're *mad.*"

"There were many experiments—I, being the first," Beecham says, as if that clears everything up. "My body does not age, but I can die like any other man. A carriage accident, or a winter chill, just as with our dear Gaspard. So, I tried to surround myself with protectors. Most did not last. The failures are burned alive; our furnace is never idle. The closest I've come are subjects who are imbued with strength, but lack the teeth. In that case, I give it to them." He smiles, knowingly. "But *you,* the son of my only escaped patient, in which the Blood of the Undamned remained dormant? That's no modern illness you've come to be treated for, Jacques. I'm particularly interested in what the cards say about *you*."

Vampire. I try to speak, but I can barely breathe.

"You've heard the tales. Read the stories."

I haven't—my parents were always folktale-averse, but I know enough from my schooling. I don't even want to entertain the notion, don't want to remember my impulses with Annie, the sick curl in my gut that forms when I think of her... my wishes to act upon them with no regard to consequence.

At this point, I'm past all reason. I begin to berate him. Threaten his life. His mother, probably long gone. His family, if he'd ever had one. His freakish experiments.

Alma jumps, startled at my outcry, and starts to sob.

"Now, now, darling," Beecham reassures her. "You're beautiful. Don't let the bad man tell you otherwise."

"My mum won't think so," Alma wails.

Beecham glances at the nurses; one of them sticks a hand through the cage. A door unlatches at my mouth, and I scream and snarl as she fits a metal contraption past my upper jaw. Then, she does the same for the bottom, securing it in place. Cranking my mouth open so wide, the skin at the sides of my lips split.

"Hush, now. We're paying her a visit soon, remember?" Beecham begins to hum a familiar tune as he enters the forceps through the wrist-sized hole.

My screams rip my throat raw. I want to fight, want to ask him what it all means, but every ounce of strength has left me. I begin to fade in and out, my entire body cranking back to life just to feel him yank the first incisor out of me.

By the time he's pulling the second tooth, my mouth is

filled with blood. I gag, letting it run down my chin so it doesn't choke me through my sobs.

Then, he tears a canine out.

The room goes cold. Spots dance at the corners of my vision, and I feel my eyes roll back into my head.

"Hurry," Beecham mutters. "Crushed Valerian root, powdered bone, and silver flakes. Then, the Vitae. Double the laudanum first."

A splash of astringent liquid coats the back of my throat, and I don't have time to choke on it, because a rough sludge is forced down my throat immediately after. The moment I sputter, my chair is tilted back so that I choke it down. It burns—it all burns, the searing pain from the raw sockets and the alcohol melding into two rods of pain, one on each side of my upper jaw.

My skull is splitting open.

I pray for the end that never seems to come quickly enough.

CHAPTER 6

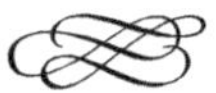

IN WHICH THE FALLEN HEIR IS TRANSFORMED, THE FURNACE BURNS BRIGHT—AND WHY HASN'T THE LAUDANUM WORN OFF YET???

*D*isappointingly, the high dose of laudanum did not seem to kill me, nor the pain. It did, however, make me *ragingly* drunk.

Better drunk than dead, I say.

I wrench myself from the cold tile floor, where I appear to sit in a dark cell. My hands fly to my face; my teeth are still missing, and I'm *freezing*. My cheeks feel like I've been standing in a draft, my chin and neck still crusted in blood.

My vision adjusts quickly in the dim light. A guard of some sort stands armed with a rifle outside the only barred exit, propped and snoring against the wall opposite the cell door just feet from me. Oil lamps flicker beyond, no sunlight to be seen.

Padded walls lined in copper mesh. A distant orange light, flickering around the corner.

In the long moment it takes me to realize I've been made prisoner, I notice the other swaying figures in the center of the room. Pale shapes, hollow-eyed. Their breathing wet, harsh, and shallow.

A woman, her face sunken, lips cracked and bloodied,

shivers in a dress of chiffon and lace now black with soot. Her throat is torn, bleeding wounds in the shape of the collar I'd worn just minutes—hours?—ago.

I'm not wholly sure they're alive, but their blood smells half sweet, half rotten. As if they're not wholly edible, but would do in a pinch.

Wow, I think, licking my lips and shuffling away until I hit the padded wall. *I am a jackass.*

My stomach growls violently in response.

A ghostly child stands close to her, and next to him, is the figure of a man crumpled upon the floor. I'm positive he's not breathing, because my pounding head has afforded me a *new* level of delirium: Whether or not I am imagining it, I can hear every sound in the room.

The whimpers of the child. The reassurances from his mother, laced in terror.

Grating metal against stone around the corner, from where the flickering orange light roars to life. Shifting stone or sediment of some sort. An iron door on poorly-oiled hinges, creaking open. Embers float into the dark after each *plop* of stone.

Through the haze, fear grips me—albeit distantly. A fucking fire.

I'm about to be incinerated, aren't I?

I begin to laugh. What else is there to do? But the sound is like sandpaper down my throat; I shove my hand into my pocket and pull out that last bag from Amah. I don't know what those cooling herbs did for me, besides probably heighten the effects of the laudanum, now that I think about it.

To give you strength when the cold tries to break you.

I am, undoubtedly, a freezing and broken man. And if I have the choice to be warmed by herbs or flame charring skin, I'll choose the first in every godforsaken lifetime.

Holding the dripping wad of fibrous herbs above my tongue, I prepare for the worst—when the child makes a ghastly noise of surprise. The man beside him has shifted a leg.

"He's alive," the boy croaks, despite his mother's desperate shushing. The skin of his mouth has been ripped at the corners, and four of his top teeth are missing, too.

"Rigors, probably," I comment, without a single thought.

As the woman cradles his head and shoots me a deadly glare, the shovelling sound around the corner stops abruptly. Terror fills her eyes, and she tugs her son closer.

"What's that noise?" the unseen presence tending to the furnace growls.

Quickly, I shove the entire wad of herbs into my mouth and nearly choke, chewing twice before swallowing it whole. If I'm lucky enough, it'll give me the fire—the strength to do something about the person approaching the strange, pale family across from me.

If I'm unlucky, it kills me. Then, none of this is my problem anymore, is it?

As soon as it's down, my body roars to life, as if a torch is lit in my chest. I place one foot under me, just as he rounds the corner and grabs the leg of the stirring man despite the hoarse protests of his family.

But the newcomer doubles back upon seeing me rise to my feet, looking like he's seen a ghost. He might as well have.

"You," I growl, sauntering across the room, my steps awkward, like a sad revenant. "Put him—"

And then... everything goes black.

PAIN BLOOMS in my right shoulder.

"Shoot it in the head, you buffoon!"

I'm halfway in the arms of the coal-shoveller, half sprawled on the floor, as if I'd fainted on him.

I make to speak, to snarl as another blast echoes throughout the room, but the sound is lost on my newly bloodied mouth; I lick my lips—it's my own blood, oozing from my bottom lip. My missing teeth are not only *there*, but lengthened into two pairs like Alma's had been. But these ones are different. Deeply rooted within me.

I stagger to my feet in shock as the woman, boy, and newly awoken man cower in the corner. My left shoulder sears in agony this time, blood splattering their faces—

But I don't spin to glance at who's shooting me, or has such poor aim, he should probably give the rifle to the kid to finish the job. I don't think about the fact that my head's one lucky shot away from being blown to smithereens.

All I can think of is what to do next.

I slam the coal-shoveller against the padded wall and sink my teeth into his throat. Deep into it. His blood is ecstacy, an instant drug to my own parched veins, singing with power. It sprays everywhere, covering me, but I swallow what I can.

The moment I feel my racing heart stop—or slow, whatever it's doing I dislike it—I'm centered. Home. Whatever has been clawing its way out of me is here now, urging me forth. What once was weakness is now adrenaline pumping through me.

I spin and punch the armored rifleman in the face, dodging his last shot. It doesn't fare too well for him; I think his skull is smashed in on the side, but there's no time to look. My gaze snaps upon the family in the corner, arms up, to show them I'm safe. Or, at least the safest thing in the sanatorium. Either way, they peel themselves off the wall; I'm at least relieved they seem more frightened by the now-dead fellow with the gun. It appears one of the man's knees have been bashed in, likely in an attempt to protect his wife and child. I scoop him up on my shoulder.

I shake the rifle free of the corpse at my feet and hand the strap to the woman, but she's frail. Bled out, and left to die on the cusp of a curse—or magic, or laudanum poisoning, or whatever it is that has brought me back to life. I wonder if they understand they're stuck in some sort of limbo, at least halfway to what I am.

I barely understand it myself.

She takes the weapon onto her shoulder and nearly collapses from its weight.

There are more footsteps echoing from above; we must be under the city. Under Beecham's.

Instinct grabs hold of me, most vile and absurd. Without thinking, I bring my palm to my mouth and slice it on my teeth. Then, I shove it in their faces, first the woman, then the boy, smearing and ensuring it's entered their mouths. I don't know what I've just done, or the life I've damned them to. All I know is, it's the best way to give them the fighting chance that was promised upon entering the infirmary.

Instead of gagging, they lap at it, their faces still wrenched in disgust—but they ingest my blood anyway, scooping it off their cheeks and onto their tongues, almost as if they cannot help themselves.

I do it to the man on my shoulder last, then bolt for the open cell door. "Hurry," I shout, beckoning for the woman and child to follow. "*Hurry!*"

I push forward into the lamplight and smash a guard and a nurse into the wall before finding the staircase they'd descended around the corner.

With the family on my tail, I ascend.

CHAPTER 7

IN WHICH HOPE IS A FILTHY WORD, LONDON IS LEFT BEHIND, AND THE HUNGER IS NO LONGER MINE ALONE TO HOLD

We climb a short ladder and emerge through a hatch that leads into a dark, seemingly abandoned storage room. It opens into one of the corridors forking off from the wide hallway we'd started in. To my ravenous disappointment, Aloysius Beecham is nowhere to be found. Neither is Alma, even as I bellow her name at a volume that rattles the floorboards.

No answer. No patients screaming for help, no more freakishly strong nurses coming to attack us. I inhale deeply, scenting the place. Empty. Not another soul, save for the still-warm bodies downstairs in that dungeon I'm convinced is unsanctioned by the city.

Sunlight is the last thing on my mind, but we pass through a ray of deep gold streaming through one of the two boarded windows at the front of the receiving room. I set the man against the wall, checking his pulse. It's low, but that won't matter soon.

I give the woman and child my name—I even tell them I'm a visiting private investigator from France. They're in obvious shock, and could do for some blood, which, with a town this large, they'll have no trouble finding. With a parting glance, I bid my strange friends adieu, and turn for the door.

You've heard the tales. Read the stories.

I understand them well enough to know that I'm either a cursed fool, or fucked in the mind… and what I don't know, I'll soon learn. I pass my hand through the ray of sunlight again. Nothing happens, but this registers belatedly, because I've run my tongue over my teeth.

My fangs are no more. In their place, smooth canines and incisors. Surely not the same ones Beecham had extracted?

There's no time to ponder the sunlight sensitivity or the way my new teeth feel in my mouth, because there are boots pounding outside and a rising swell of angry voices. Hastily, I untuck my shirt and wipe at least my mouth clean—and throw the door open to a full swarm of constables, some on horses, some with pistols, each wearing that particularly irking look of righteousness and feigned concern.

I raise my hands indulgently. "Gentlemen." My voice is so smooth, it shocks me. "I don't know if anyone's informed you, but within these very doors, a certain Aloysius Ermengarde Beecham the Third has been performing crimes against God, science, and man. He's also broken at *least* three sections of the Hippocratic Oath."

They remain rooted in place, exchanging wary glances.

"You might find some survivors inside, or not. But you should look, just to be sure. Diligence and all."

And, with that, I saunter south on Gill Street, much too high on my freedom from that claustrophobic infirmary—and possibly still laudanum—to care what passersby are whispering about my torn, bloodied attire.

It's not long before the autumn afternoon is filled with bellowing screams and more gunshots. I should be fleeing the scene, or burning down the building, or maybe even mourning, but the only thing I run *to* is the one I want to save.

All I can think of is her. Seamstress and part-time shop runner at Lewis & Allenby's. Possible accomplice to my enemy. Love of my godforsaken life.

It seems most of the town has flocked down to Gill after hearing the commotion. By the time I turn onto Limehouse Causeway, the only sign of life there is Annie, who bursts into the road just in time, flinging Amah's door wide open.

All it takes is one look and the uptick of her hammering heart, and my teeth elongate, the tips pulsing into my bottom lip.

The unmistakable timing with my erection is comical. There's probably some correlation there.

I'm instantly sobered when she tugs out a travel trunk more than half the size of her body and heaves it onto the sidewalk. Her face is blotchy as she glances about the other shops before her gaze comes to rest on me.

"Annie." I approach her urgently—but slow, startled, the moment I realize her face is splattered with blood. The tips of her fingers are smeared in red.

The slap that cracks across my face echoes off the surrounding buildings.

"*You did this to me,*" she snarls through her tears. There are no fangs—not yet—but the hunger I'd seen in myself the night before blazes through her eyes, wild and ravenous as they comb me.

My torn, bloodstained garments. My teeth.

"What have you—" She glances down at her hands, trembling violently. "What have I done?" She looks more pissed than afraid, but she also doesn't come any closer.

Merde. I stagger back, uncomprehending. I hadn't been... *this*... when we'd made love. Hadn't bitten her, though God knows I'd wanted to. We'd been careful.

Unable to help myself, I reach for her; Annie stumbles back, nearly tripping over the travel trunk and staring into the open apartment.

Amah braces herself in the doorway. Blood darkens the collar of her white blouse while one of her hands clutches her side. Her glazed eyes find her granddaughter's, then mine. Then, they lower, perhaps not wanting to see what I've become.

"She needs help." Annie looks like she's ready to fall to her knees. "I didn't mean to—I got so angry when she said she'd sent you off. I lost control. I don't know what came over me."

She then turns to vomit in the street.

Annie somehow understands what's happened to me, yet doesn't recognize the striking resemblance in her own violence.

"Oh, I think I do."

Her eyes flash at my response, just as I turn and catch Amah just as she collapses against the doorframe. She's still conscious, the wounds at her neckline and ribs, shallow from what I can tell. She must be shaken.

"I asked you to stay." Annie wipes her mouth on her sleeve. "I was trying to protect you!"

"So you knew nothing of this?" My gaze pins her, dragging from her face to her throat. My fangs have started to throb, and all I can think of is tasting her. It's almost as if she can sense it too, because I *feel* her fighting her instincts. "You didn't know what you were protecting me from?"

"I thought you were wanted for some sort of crime. An unpaid bill, or an unfinished operation."

"So you were fine with me potentially getting my kneecaps

shattered, but growing fangs and a deep craving for your blood is where you draw the line?" I want to lunge. To pin her against the wall in my betrayal and hunger. The only thing keeping me anchored is the shivering old woman clinging to my waist.

Annie's silence speaks volumes.

"Your grandmother believed it was a good idea either way."

"You don't understand what Beecham promised her," Annie snaps. "What it meant to someone like her. Legal standing, protection for the shop. I didn't care *what* he'd approached her for—I agreed to help. To send an incoming inspector his way, until you came into my shop. And I *tried* to get you to leave. To leave me alone." Tears of hatred form at the corners of her eyes. "Amah didn't mean any harm. She didn't mean it. She didn't mean to hurt you."

She says it as if to convince herself.

I look pointedly down at the travel trunk behind her. "Then why were you running?"

Just then, Amah grunts against me and straightens. She blinks up at me from under my arm, her lashes as long as her granddaughter's. "Oh. It's you."

"Yes," I snarl. "*Me.*"

Amah sighs and pulls a sachet from her pocket, and tilts her head back before emptying it into her mouth. Then, she straightens, and dusts herself off. "I sent you because I knew you'd be the end of that place."

Annie's lips part, but no sound comes.

Suddenly, the street behind us erupts in a chorus of shouts, the shrill bark of a constable's whistle and heavy hoofbeats. *He went this way! Onward!*

They're close, much too close for my liking. Their search will inevitably lead them here. I won't have them swarm Limehouse, especially these shops and homes.

They're close enough that Annie and Amah can hear them, too.

Annie watches my face shift as I deliberate, and as I do—a harbor bell rings in the distance. She sees what's coming a heartbeat too late.

"Don't you dare," she hisses, backing away.

But I lunge and catch her around the waist, scooping her up effortlessly and tossing her over my shoulder. She thrashes, cussing, boots kicking the air, her nails raking across my cheek.

Calmly, I bend and grab the trunk handle. She's just as beautiful when she's furious.

"You can't do this!" Annie shouts. "Where are you taking me?"

There is no easy answer. All I know is that she, and her Amah, will never be without my protection. Not with Beecham still out there. Not with things like *me* out there.

"To the docks. We've got a ship to catch." I glance down and hold out my free arm. "Can you walk, Amah?"

The old woman smiles up at me. "For now."

VIIMORTE

ANNIE

IN WHICH THERE IS NO TIME TO EXPLAIN

The docks reek of piss and brine, a vile concoction that clings to the evening fog and settles in my throat with every ragged breath I take. It is bitter and unrelenting, but none more than the brute I writhe against. The *beast* who has slung me over his shoulder.

I scream his name as loud as I can. "Jacques! Put me down this instant!"

My voice is shrill, echoing off the water, startling a seagull into flight and deafening every poor sailor within a half-mile radius. But I don't care, and neither does Jacques. He doesn't stop—he doesn't even slow down. He continues marching along as I bounce across his shoulder, hauled off like a sack of grain, my skirts flailing around me disgracefully.

"You *monster*," I wheeze, trying to twist, but Jacques holds my hips steady. I jerk, blinding myself with the sweltering autumn sun in its reflected descent. I'm forced to turn towards the street of wary, soot-dusted onlookers who don't lift a single finger or voice to help me. They're too tired, too poor, too sick to help a woman like me. I suppose that's the jarring irony of a place like London. "Put me down this instant!"

Finally, my boot connects with something: a passing barrel, or his ribs, hopefully. It takes him a moment, but he grunts. The sound is in amusement rather than pain.

"Stop squirming," he advises over his shoulder, much too calmly for a man being physically assaulted, and I wish to once more draw blood across the cheek that keeps healing. Doing so might draw more attention than necessary, or invoke whatever demon has made its home in his skin.

I don't want him stabbed, or hung, or imprisoned—not that I'm sure it would do anything. But a solid mugging, on top of being set down upon my own two feet, would suffice.

"You'll fall into the Thames, and I'm not jumping in after you."

"Good," I snap, unease blooming in my stomach as I consider Beatrice and Elias. They're still in Scotland, and won't be back another week. Without me, Thomas will be lost; poor old man, *what will he be without me?* I'm not even sure he remembers how to unlock the front door. "I hope the river swallows me whole. I'll haunt you for the rest of your miserable undead—*oof!*"

The last of my dignity is sucked out of me, along with my breath as he slows, adjusting me on his shoulder.

Behind us, Amah is talking to someone, our travel trunk in-hand. Her voice is smooth and unbothered as she explains something to a dockhand maybe several years older than my mother—Southern China, or the Philippines, or Indonesia, maybe—whose friendly eyes widen. At that moment, Jacques stills beneath me, his jaw tightening against my side into a reflexive grimace.

Or a smile, I can't tell which.

The man nods as my grandmother murmurs to him, hands him a few coins, and exchanges a quick glance with

Jacques. I'm not sure what the look was, but I'm distracted by the way the man grins—*grins*, as if he's just been told I'm merely suffering a fit of feminine hysteria and not, in fact, being abducted in broad daylight.

He puts two fingers to his mouth, and whistles up the gangway at his feet; I'm so furious, I haven't noticed the two-masted vessel beside him. Amah beckons us over, and Jacques too readily obliges.

I ready myself, placing my palms against the backs of Jacques's shoulders, preparing for him to lower me. He'll place me down—surely he does not mean as he says—and I'll make my esc—

"Congratulations, on your engagement!" the man proclaims, tipping his hat at Jacques. "My, that's a beautiful fiancé you've got there."

Every muscle in my aching, sweat-slicked body freezes. "I am *not* his—*his*—!" On second thought, he does deserve the gallows. "This is *illegal*! Someone arrest him!"

No one does. A few of the vessel's crew glance over, but they look far more entertained than alarmed. One chuckles as another mutters, "She's got fire, that one."

"Is she what happened to you?" another asks, leaning over the side and eyeing the blood covering Jacques's torn shirt and the burgundy crust all over my fingertips. They're seamen. They must be used to brawls. I redden and tuck my hands under me.

Jacques only laughs through his nose, though his shoulders remain unamusedly rigid. "There is no time to explain." He cranes his head behind us, as if watching for someone, and somehow manages a gracious, almost trained bow. "May I?"

As the dockhand returns the gesture and unhooks the chain, I rear back and drive my elbow square into the back of

Jacques's neck. He flinches, finally. *"There.* That was your spine. Do you want me to crack it in two?"

He doesn't answer me, not aloud. But I feel the shift in his body, the tightening of his grip around the backs of my legs, his fingers shifting away from my ass. The way his breath hitches before he exhales through his nose like I'm some tantruming child.

I despise how solid he feels beneath me, how unshakable. I despise the heat encompassing my throat and rising in my chest, not entirely from rage.

Amah is beside us, watching my face contort with that awful serene expression of hers, the one that makes it clear she's orchestrating something far greater than my comprehension will allow. She gives the dockhand a few more coins and a wink that could pass for a thanks or something else entirely—and then meets my eye with the satisfaction of a woman who just pulled off a social miracle.

"Thank you for doing this for us," she says to the dockhand.

"Of course, Madame Tan. It's nice to see you, and again, I'm so sorry about Grace and John."

I glare at her through hot tears as she follows us up. *A ship.* After all we'd been through, after everything she'd told me about. After all she'd weathered.

"I told him you were Jacques's betrothed as of this morning, and had suffered a nervous collapse as a result. The physician suggested an immediate exposure to sea air, and that a train ride to one of those stuffy ferries would worsen your symptoms. What?" she says quietly at my expression of dumbfounded rage, as if this is a perfectly reasonable explanation to being dragged across the Channel without one's consent. "They're a supply ship headed to Calais tomorrow. People make allowances for love."

I growl, writhing again to no effect. *"This* isn't love."

Not yet, Amah's stoic expression says.

The gangplank groans beneath us as Jacques takes the final step. The deck opens around us, a blur of shadows—ropes the size of my arm, sails, tar-stained planks, and the heavy scent of salt and oil.

I go still, for just a moment.

I think of Beatrice and Elias, soon on their way back from Scotland to find the shop empty—Thomas, clueless; I think of our apartment on the Causeway, the shops that line it. Our friendly, assessing neighbors who live there, those who brought us food and tea when Amah and I spent an entire season grieving. The sanctuary of my bedroom, and the man who glimpsed a long-hidden part of my soul within its cozy confines. A taste of what I'd been missing, the life never meant for me.

It hits me all at once: I am not getting off this ship. I glance over the side where the water glitters, dark and gold in the setting sun.

And then, as if sensing the shift in my thoughts, Jacques finally speaks. His voice vibrates my abdomen, low and just for me. "I'll put you down when it's safe."

Safe. I could laugh. I could scream. Instead, I say nothing at all.

Because the vessel is pulling away from the dock. Because the shore is quickly disappearing, the mist of the Thames swallowing the crowd and chimneys and everything I'd ever known.

Because, for the first time in my life, I can't see what's ahead of us—and, God help me, I don't think I want to.

Dear Reader,

If you find yourself confused, that's fair. If you're aroused, that's also fair.

Fret not—Beecham's still out there, Alma's still hysterical and bent on searching for her parents. Something dreadful is happening to Annie indeed.

Our narrator's certainly a menace.

You can expect Book Two of the *My Darling Malady* series very soon, with more blood, worse decisions, and at least one heartfelt apology that is interrupted by gunfire.

THE CRIMSON COMPENDIUM

AS NOTED IN BOOK IV: PART II OF THE HISTORIES OF THE LASTING NIGHT

Disclaimer: <u>Don't Be Stupid.</u>

The plants in this Compendium are for vampires, Daemons, and other arcane creatures with too much heat in their bellies and not enough sense in their heads. If you are mortal and soft, do not eat them unless you know what you are doing. Which, you don't.

Exception: Ginger.

If your belly is cold, or there's a scratch to your throat, a little ginger won't harm you. Too much of anything will sour the senses, but at least you'll stay human (most likely).

Everything else, keep your tongue off it.

- Amah Joy

Guī bǎn → 龜板 → Turtle Shell Plastron. Cold. Used in rituals to preserve the soul, prolong humanity in vampirism.

Bái sháo → 白芍 → White Peony Root. Slightly Cold. Slows transformation, dampens hunger, lust, grief. A "bridging herb" that encourages emotional continuity between states.

Dān shēn → 丹參 → Red Sage Root. Slightly Cold. Calms the heart fire, may delay* transformation and smoothen the process. Breaks up stagnancy in the blood. *May accelerate vampirism if used in large amounts.

Fùzǐ → 附子 → Aconite. Hot, **Toxic**. Accelerates arcane transformation by forcefully reviving dying Yang.

Diānqié → 顛茄 → Mad Eggplant. Cold, **Toxic**. Masks* transformation by inhibiting parasympathetic functions, dulling hunger, and sedating bloodlust. **May accelerate the transformation process by killing the patient.**

Ginger Root → 薑 → Jiāng. Warm. Accelerates blood movement. Can be used in donors or victims to enhance the vampire's feeding efficiency, flavor, or to resuscitate a dying Fledgling just long enough for transformation to take hold.

LEXIQUE DE TRADUCTION

As you may have noticed, Jacques occasionally lapses into French—sometimes in fury, sometimes in passion, and never in a way particularly helpful to non-Francophones (or to those actively opposed to them). Indeed, this was no accident. The petty obstruction was deliberate, crafted by Monsieur Valmont himself to vex you as surely as he vexes Annie.

It has since dawned on me, your ever-dutiful and, I daresay, kindhearted author, that paperback readers lack the built-in translation feature available on most e-readers. To remedy this, I've updated all editions, print and digital (including Kindle Unlimited), to include a lexicon of Jacques-isms for quick reference. You may also find the full lexicon on the following page.

LEXIQUE DE TRADUCTION

Jacques's Musings	Translation
Ah, oui. Car rien n'exprime l'urgence morale comme l'héritage d'une propriété à Marylebone.	Ah, yes. For nothing expresses moral urgency quite like inheriting a property in Marylebone.
D'après le journal quotidien, les Parlementaires demeurent un chef de file mondial en matière de science et de médecine en progrès. Apparemment.	According to the daily newspaper, Parliamentarians remain world leaders in science and medical progress. *Apparently.*
Quelle petite sotte.	What a silly girl.
Tu oses me braver ainsi.	You dare to defy me like this.
Je vais t'arracher les yeux et te les enfoncer dans la gorge.	I'm going to rip your eyes out and shove them down your throat.

ACKNOWLEDGMENTS

To my wonderfully talented editors and critique partners, Jessica, Cydney, Holly. Special thanks to my author friends and colleagues, Kiara Alexander-Castro, (*The Heir & The Knight*), Sean Gibson (*The Part About the Dragon Was [Mostly] True* and *The Camelot Shadow*), Chris Patrick Carolan (*The Nightshade Cabal*), and C. Vonzale Lewis (*Lineage*, *Zealot*, and *Descendants of the Big House*), whose generosity in reading an unpolished copy and invaluable advice have enriched this tale greatly. From history to linguistics, your feedback illuminates the dark corners of Beecham's Infirmary.

And by that, I mean haunts them further. I'm so grateful.

To my incredible narration team, Christopher Tester, Krys Janae, and Daniele Lanzarotta: Thanks for entertaining me when I mentioned I was bringing an old short story back to life. Your voice and engineering talents make the storytelling process so surreal; thank you for sharing them with Jacques, Annie, and Amah Joy.

Tim, my husband, best friend, and in-house historian: thank you for being the constant, persevering fire one might find in a simmering kiss under the eaves of a countryside manor—or in the ghostly ruins of an abandoned sanatorium. Thank you for your wit, encouragement, and steadfast support. I love you.

And to you, Dear Reader. Thank you for strolling the streets of London with us, and joining Jacques and Annie on their haphazard adventure. The mystery isn't solved yet—in fact, it's barely begun.

The next installment of the *My Darling Malady* series will contain a stroke of luck, Parisian adventure, and a most unfortunate case of seasickness. Until then.

Yours in shadowed contemplation,
Briar Somerset

Briar Somerset is the author of *The A Lay of Ruinous Reign* series (a Vampire Romantasy steeped in Breton folklore and Arthurian legend), and the *My Darling Malady* series—a collection of Gaslamp Gothic Paranormal Romance novellas following the unfortunate adventures of a reluctant investigator and seamstress through the shadowed byways of Victorian society.

Somerset is an enthusiastic enjoyer of fantasy RPGs/TTRPGs, scalding cups of tea, and finding whimsy in the macabre.

In all facets of her craft, Somerset enjoys exploring the—*disenchanting*, if you will—undertones of history, romance, and the arcane.

instagram.com/authorbriarsomerset

www.ingramcontent.com/pod-product-compliance
Lightning Source LLC
Chambersburg PA
CBHW061919130726
47908CB00017B/2570